Never Been
Kissed

Books by Melody Carlson

Never Been Kissed

A Novel

Melody Carlson

Revell

a division of Baker Publishing Group
Grand Rapids, Michigan

© 2011 by Melody Carlson

Published by Revell
a division of Baker Publishing Group
P.O. Box 6287, Grand Rapids, MI 49516-6287
www.revellbooks.com

Printed in the United States of America

Library of Congress Cataloging-in-Publication Data
Carlson, Melody.
    Never been kissed : a novel / Melody Carlson.
        p.   cm.
    Summary: Sixteen-year-old Elise thinks starting her new high school knowing popular Asher will make things easier but not only does she develop a crush on him, she gets on the wrong side of his girlfriend and finds herself accused of "sexting."
    ISBN 978-0-8007-3259-2 (pbk.)
    [1. Interpersonal relations—Fiction. 2. High schools—Fiction. 3. Schools—Fiction. 4. Moving, Household—Fiction. 5. Text messages (Telephone systems)—Fiction. 6. Christian life—Fiction.] I. Title.
PZ7.C216637Ndv 2011
[Fic]—dc22   2010027113

11 12 13 14 15 16 17   7 6 5 4 3 2 1

1

"You're kidding, right?" Stacie's brows lift and her eyes widen with suspicion.

"Of course," I assure her. "Totally pulling your leg."

She laughs loudly. "Because for a minute I thought you were serious, Elise. Even though you don't look like the kind of girl who's *never* been kissed, you had me going."

I try to make my laughter sound genuine. "Yeah, well, you're an easy mark." Unfortunately, I was actually trying to be honest with her just now. But it's obvious she doesn't want the truth from me. She prefers fascinating fiction to the boring facts of my real life. Even so, I feel a little guilty for the way I've been stringing her along.

"So, back to the subject, Elise. What *are* you going to do for your sixteenth birthday?"

I stare down at my colorful toenails. Stacie decided we needed to give ourselves pedicures, and we've been experimenting with nail polish colors. The result is a carnival on my right foot. I just can't decide between funky limelight, flirty fuchsia, perky purple, or punchy pink. "I don't know," I say as I wiggle my toes in the sunlight. "Which color do you like best?"

She squints at my toes. "Maybe you should stick with the rainbow look and just do your other foot the same. And here's some electric blue for your pinkie. But I was talking about your birthday, Elise, not your toenails. Sixteen is big. A lot of girls around here pull out the stops with their sweet sixteen parties."

"Is that what you're going to do?" I ask her as I reach for the electric blue.

"Well, that's a ways off," she admits. "But maybe. Yeah, sure, why not? I think I'll have a huge party—maybe rent a ballroom and hire a band and have a Hummer stretch limo drop me off like I'm a celebrity—and of course I'll be wearing a really great dress."

I just nod like I believe this. But the truth is I don't think either of us—Stacie or I—are likely to have one of those over-the-top sweet sixteen parties. Furthermore, I don't even want one. Oh, maybe I would want one . . . in a perfect world. But I don't live in a perfect world. And neither does Stacie.

We live in the Tropicana Suites on Alejandro Drive on the not-so-cool side of town. Both of our moms are single and "financially challenged." Currently, Stacie's mom is between jobs, and my mom struggles just to make ends meet. Or so she likes to say, and way too much as far as I'm concerned.

So, seriously, a sweet sixteen party is pretty much out of the question for both of us. Besides that, Stacie, who's only going to be a freshman, won't even be fifteen for a few months, so her sixteenth birthday isn't really an issue.

I don't normally hang with girls who are younger than me . . . but nothing about this summer has been very normal. I guess I should be glad that it's almost over, except for the prospect of going to a new high school. That, combined with Stacie—a fourteen-year-old—as my only friend, fills me with a deep sense of dread.

"So who kissed you anyway?" Stacie asks as she splashes her feet in the pool. This rather compact swimming pool is situated in the center of our retro (meaning old and run-down) apartment complex. But the pool is actually the one perk of this otherwise pathetic property. At least when there's not some skanky party going on down here. But Mr. Galloway has been doing his best to make sure the tenants adhere to the "bathing suits required" rule lately. And I heard that Joey Feducci has been given notice, which has my mom greatly relieved. Joey is this middle-aged dude who thinks he's God's gift to women and hits on any female within whistling distance, including my mom and me, which is so disgusting . . . I can't even go there.

"Elise?" Stacie is peering at me. "Hello?"

"Huh?" I look up from where I'm hunched over, finishing up the electric blue polish on my right pinky toe.

"*Who* kissed you?"

"Oh." I sit up straight, pasting my "I'm so much older than you" expression on my face. "You mean the first time, right?"

"How many times *have* you been kissed?"

I narrow my eyes and give her a mysterious smile—just like I've seen B do on *Gossip Girl*. "Wouldn't *you* like to know?"

She nods. "Yeah, I would. How many times?"

Now, I'm not usually inclined to telling fibs. But I'm also not inclined to opening myself up to unnecessary teasing from this fourteen-year-old. I seriously doubt that she's ever been kissed either. I mean, between her braces, which she really needs to brush a bit more diligently, and her complexion, which I've told her might improve if she just washed her face once in a while, plus her totally absent breasts . . . well, let's just say that not many boys have been knocking down her door.

Not that this gives me the right to deceive her, but I happen to be blessed with an excellent imagination. In fact, it's this kind of creative outlet that probably keeps me from totally losing it. Because sometimes it feels like my imagination is about all I have. So what does it hurt if I tell a whopper now and then? If nothing else, I'm providing Stacie and myself with some cheap entertainment on a boring hot August afternoon.

"Come on," she urges me, "spill the beans. I'm waiting."

I stick my feet into the lukewarm pool water and sigh as if I'm trying to remember all the juicy details of my love life. "Well, let's see. The *first* kiss . . . it was from Allen Brewster when I was thirteen, and it was at—"

"Seriously, your first kiss was thirteen?"

I kind of shrug. "I was *almost* thirteen."

She giggles as she splashes some water on her arms. "What was it like?"

I consider this and come up empty. "It was, like, a kiss."

"Duh. But what did it feel like? Was it soggy or mushy—was there tongue involved?"

I roll my eyes and try not to be grossed out as I lean back. Taking in a long breath, I place my hands on the cement behind me and stretch my neck so that my long hair tickles the bare part of my back. "Well, it was slightly wet," I tell her, "and no tongue was involved, thank you very much."

"And so . . . ?" She waits eagerly.

"Then there was Jake Richey," I continue with mock confidence to hide my guilt. "I was almost fourteen when we got together. We went out from the end of eighth grade clear into my sophomore year." I continue to describe this boy in explicit detail. This is something I'm not making up—I mean how he looked and acted and everything. Because Jake was a real guy and he was totally hot. But he didn't know that I even existed, at least not back in eighth grade. The girl he went with all those years was a stuck-up cheerleader named Jocelyn Matthews. She was one of those perky, plucky blondes who acted like she was sweet and nice when anyone "worthwhile" was looking, but at other times she loved to pick on girls like me. I suspect it was simply to boost her self-esteem. Or maybe she was just bored. Whatever her reasons, the girl had a mean streak.

That was probably my excuse for fantasizing about her boyfriend. Like it was my way to get even with Jocelyn. Consequently, I daydreamed about Jake on a fairly regular basis during middle school. I would imagine stealing him from Jocelyn—breaking her cold, hard heart. But I wasn't only about retaliation, because Jake was actually a cool guy. And even though he didn't know my name, he never did anything mean or hurtful to me. Sometimes I'd see him stand up for someone else who was being picked on. So, naturally, one of my favorite escapes from my pathetic reality was to hope that one day Jake would actually look my way, really see me, and even take a genuine interest in me. Sometimes I even believed it was possible.

In fact, it almost happened last year when some other mean girl, not Jocelyn, tripped me on my way into Geometry class. My arms were filled with my bag and books, and when I went *splat* on the floor, my stuff went everywhere like a yard sale, and while everyone else was laughing, Jake came over and helped me gather up my junk. I think I might've mumbled an embarrassed "thanks," and then he looked straight into my eyes and said, "No problem." I seriously thought I was going to melt into a great big puddle.

Unfortunately, the school year was almost finished by then, so my big plan for the future was that I'd reinvent myself during the summer and show up at the beginning of my junior year as the new and improved Elise Storton. I would get Jake's attention and he would totally get over stupid Jocelyn, and we'd start dating, fall in love, go to prom, attend college together, eventually marry, get a dog, and maybe even have children someday.

But then Mom decided to take a "better" job, and that meant moving to a town about forty miles away from my old high school. So here I am stuck in the Tropicana Suites, telling Stacie lies about my past. Yes, I am a loser. My life is pathetic. And I'm halfway tempted to cut the bull and tell Stacie the truth—the whole, ugly truth. Yet she eats up my stories, and I'm sure she has a lot more fun listening to my make-believe life than she'd have hearing the real deal, which would probably just depress us both so badly that we'd need therapy or medication or start smoking dope or something equally disgusting. So, really, I'm doing her a favor.

"Why don't you and Jake still get together? I mean Renaldo's not that far away. Can't he drive over here to visit?"

"He could . . . except that we sort of broke up," I tell her.

"Why?" Stacie looks seriously disturbed by this news.

Since I've been pretty much telling the story of Jake and Jocelyn, I decide to continue. "Well, it was the end of the school year, and this older guy, a senior, was really into me . . . and he was actually a pretty cool guy. Jake started getting jealous . . . and that's when I decided I'd outgrown that relationship. Time to move on. Poor Jake, I think he's still not over me."

"But you're over him?" She looks dubious.

"Yeah, what with moving away and all . . . I decided it really was time for a clean break."

"So what about the senior dude? Where's he? Why doesn't he come over here and take you out?"

"Well, it turned out Micah wasn't as into me as I thought." I kind of laugh as I remember Jocelyn going around looking all miserable and brokenhearted toward the end of the school year. So much so that I suspect Jake has taken her back by now. Not that I care. I so don't. "Anyway, after we moved here, I decided to take a vacation from guys. When school starts, I'll just find someone new."

"It must be so easy for you." Stacie shakes her head.

"What do you mean?"

She turns and looks at me with a longing expression. "You're so pretty. Guys probably fall all over themselves to date you."

This totally shocks me. "Seriously? You think I'm pretty?"

She rolls her eyes. "Duh." Then she reaches over and holds a strand of my hair in her hands, flicking it in my face. "Your hair is so long and silky you could probably be in a Pantene ad."

"Well . . . thanks." Now I feel kind of guilty for lying to her.

"You've got perfect skin and a great body." She scowls. "In fact, you remind me of my sister Leslie."

"I didn't know you have a sister."

"She's twenty and pretty and I hate her."

I kind of laugh. "That's too bad."

"It's just not fair." She scowls again as she throws one of her rubber flip-flops into the pool, watching as it floats to the middle. "Why can't I be pretty too?"

"Hey, you're going to be pretty someday," I assure her. "Especially if you take better care of your teeth with those braces. And you've got really nice eyes, Stacie. I'd gladly trade my hazel ones for your blue. And your hair would be great if you used a little conditioner after you swim— chlorine and blonde hair really don't mix. Honestly, I'll bet you're one of those girls who's going to be a knockout in a few years."

"Yeah, right. Even if that was true, it doesn't do me any good right now."

"Sure it does," I assure her. "This is a good time to work on your inner beauty." Okay, I cannot believe I just said that. It's exactly what my mom used to say to me when I felt plain and ugly.

She laughs. "Right. Inner beauty. Now that's something most guys are really looking for."

I consider this. "I'll bet some of them are. But it's probably the quiet ones, you know, the ones who are actually nice."

She brightens. "You think so?"

I nod then stand. "Yep. I know so." I dive into the pool and am surprised at how cold it feels on my sun-baked head. As I swim underwater to the other side, which is possible to do with one breath because the pool is so short, I imagine that I'm a mermaid (kind of like Ariel) and that when I pop my head out of the water, at the other end a gorgeous guy (kind of like Eric) will be waiting. Okay, I know that's pretty juvenile and so silly I'd never admit it to anyone. But, hey, it's *my* daydream!

2

"You'll stay at Grandma's while I'm in Seattle for the convention," Mom tells me on Saturday night. Part of Mom's new job managing a small chain of gift shops is to attend conventions to purchase merchandise, and this is her first trip. It's just one week until school starts, and I'd been fantasizing that she might actually take me with her, imagining that I'd do some back-to-school shopping in the city and that we'd have this really great time together. Naturally the bottom line, aka the almighty dollar, put the brakes on that little plan.

"Why can't I stay here on my own?" I ask her.

"Because you're not old enough, Elise. I've told you that dozens of times already."

"When *will* I be old enough?"

Mom pauses from packing her suitcase to frown at me. "Maybe when you're seventeen."

"Seventeen?" I pound her pillow with my fist. "That's crazy. You were practically married by then."

She makes a face at me. "And that turned out real great, didn't it?"

It's no secret that my parents got married because they had to. Mom got pregnant with me in her senior year of high school. Thinking that she was so grown up and that my dad, in his second year of college, was so mature, they married. My mom placed me in day care and worked at a variety of retail jobs that helped put my dad through school (after his parents bailed on him due to his choice to father a child and take a wife). Shortly after he graduated with some computer degree, he dumped Mom and me for this chick he'd been sleeping with all through college.

I hated him for a while, but then I became a Christian when I was twelve and eventually realized my need to forgive him—for my sake as much as for his. And I have to give the guy credit, at least he pays child support—although my mom (or the state) would have his head on a platter if he didn't. In exchange, I try not to bug him, which he appreciates since he has his own precious life with Arianna and their two little boys. Hey, just because I forgave him doesn't mean I have to like him.

I fold Mom's navy blue warm-ups and hand them to her. She always takes these on her trips to relax in.

"Thanks, honey," she tells me. "I really do wish I could afford to take you with me, but money's so tight right now."

"Yeah, right." I try not to roll my eyes. But, seriously, she says this like every other day.

"So have you decided what you want for your birthday?" she asks.

"You mean besides a life?"

She laughs. "Oh, Elise, you'll have a life once school starts."

"Right. I can hardly wait. The only person I know is Stacie, and she's, well, she's nice . . . but she's not very cool, and besides, she's only a freshman."

"You'll make other friends too."

I hand her pink rubber flip-flops to her. She uses them as slippers in hotels because she worries about the germs and gunk that might be in the carpets.

"Anyway, my flight is in the morning and Grandma will be by in the afternoon to pick you up. She's really looking forward to it, Elise."

I brighten slightly. I actually like my grandmother a lot. And I've probably missed her as much as anything else after moving here. But I suspect it's been a healthy move for Mom since Grandma always had this tendency to tell her how to live, which was somewhat understandable considering we lived in a guest house on Grandma's property.

Sometimes I felt sorry for my mom when we lived there. It seemed like she never had a chance to really grow up completely. Between my dad's dumping her and my grandma's controlling her, it's kind of like she got stuck somewhere along the line. She never really had much of a life—no friends, no dates, no interests. Nothing much besides her work and me and her parents. Although sometimes I wondered if it was actually her choice. Maybe it was her way of protecting herself. Or perhaps she was simply married to her job.

Anyway, I had actually hoped that this move—and having some space away from her mother—might encourage my mom to start dating again. Not that I want her to get married or anything too serious. At least not while I'm still living at home. But maybe someday. Because I really do hate to think of her being lonely after I leave.

"I wish you had your license," Mom tells me as we stand outside the apartment complex, waiting for the taxi to arrive to take her to the airport. "Then you could just drop me off."

"Hey, I'm totally willing to drive you—"

"No way," she says. "You know that's illegal. But the sooner you get your license, the happier I'll be." Just then the taxi arrives and she kisses me on the cheek as the driver loads her luggage in the trunk. "Be good," she tells me as she waves goodbye.

Like I have any alternatives? But I just nod and smile. Then she's gone and I'm home alone for a few hours. First I pack up my stuff for Grandma's, then I use the remaining time to catch up on my sleep (by the pool) as well as my tan, which is looking pretty good. Stacie never shows up by the pool, but I suspect it's because she's mad at me today.

"The last week of summer vacation and you have to go off to your grandma's house," she complained yesterday.

"It's not like I have a choice in the matter," I told her.

"You could've stayed at my place," she said with a pout.

I explained that I haven't seen much of my grandma since moving here, and also that my grandpa died last winter and my grandma has been pretty lonely. But I could tell that Stacie's nose was still out of joint. I chalk this up to immaturity and promise myself to find an older best friend when school starts.

"There you are," my grandma calls out as she enters the pool area. "All ready to go?"

"Just let me put on some clothes," I tell her as I grab my towel and my library book.

She hugs me then looks me up and down. "Well, Elise, you're looking prettier than ever. But watch out for that sun. I hear that skin cancer is on the rise."

"I use sunscreen," I tell her as we go upstairs. Of course, I don't tell her that it's not a very good sunscreen, because when it comes to grandmas, ignorance is usually bliss.

She chuckles. "I suppose I'm not one to talk when I think of how I used to get burned as a teen. Can you believe your old grandmother used to wear a bikini?"

I laugh and then remind her, like I always do, that fifty-five is not terribly old for a grandmother. In fact, I've had friends with moms about that same age.

We gather up my things and load them into her old Cadillac, and she hands me the car keys. "I've decided that you'll be the driver this week," she tells me as we get in the car. "I'm on vacation."

I smile as I start the car. "That's fine with me. I need to log some more hours to get my driver's license anyway."

"I've also decided to give you your birthday present early," she tells me as I slow down for a light.

"Cool. What is it?"

"Back-to-school shopping."

"Seriously?"

"Yes. Your mom mentioned that you haven't gotten much yet, and I know that money's tighter than usual. I was thinking about how you'll be going to a new school, and I think you should put your best foot forward. So we're going all out, Elise. Tomorrow we'll hit the mall and we'll shop till we drop."

"Way cool," I tell her. Suddenly I'm very glad I didn't stay home alone after all.

It's fun to be back on my old stomping ground too. Although I do find myself wishing we'd never moved and that I could return to life as I knew it. Back when I had a life.

Still, I decide to make the best of it and even offer to walk my grandma's schnauzer, Millie. Dog and I slowly cruise the old neighborhood, finally stopping in the park, where I run into my old friend Hilary Linder. She has a dog with her too, her mom's new and slightly neurotic poodle, Fifi.

"Elise," she cries when she sees me. "What are you doing here?" I explain about visiting Grandma, then we hug like we were better friends than we actually were. We let the dogs off their leashes, and she immediately tells me she has a new boyfriend.

"Really?" I ask in surprise, since Hilary, like me, wasn't exactly date bait last year.

"Do you remember Monroe Gordon?" she asks.

"Not exactly," I admit.

"Well, he's kind of a quiet guy," she says. "He was my lab partner in Chemistry and—"

"Oh yeah," I say. "I do remember him. He seemed nice."

She smiles and nods. "He is nice."

"Anyway, he has a cousin who goes to Garfield High."

"Really?"

"Yeah." She frowns as if thinking. "I think his name is Ashton . . . No, that's not right. But it's close. And his last name is Gordon like Monroe's because their dads are brothers."

"Oh." I nod like this is of interest to me, but the truth is I don't really care. I mean, what are the chances I'll actually meet this Ashton-whatever-his-name-is or, even if I did, that he'd be someone I'd want to know? Especially if he's anything like his cousin, because as I recall, Monroe is kind of nerdy.

"Wouldn't that be cool if you got together with him?"

I smile like I think it'd be cool, although I know it's pretty unlikely.

"We could go out together sometime," she continues. "You know, on a double date."

We chat some more and then Hilary looks at her watch and announces that she's got to hurry home to get ready for a big date tonight. "How long are you staying at your grandmother's?" she calls out as we're heading our separate ways.

"Until Friday."

"I'll call you, okay?"

"Okay," I shout back. But as I walk Millie back to Grandma's, I'm betting that Hilary won't call. I have a feeling she's pretty wrapped up in her new boyfriend. And really, I'm happy for her. Yet I do wonder . . . would I possibly have had a boyfriend too—that is, if I hadn't been uprooted and moved away from here?

Shopping ends up being pretty fun, and Grandma, as always, is a lot easier to shop with than my mom. Not that she just hands me over her credit cards or anything like that, but she's a lot more generous than Mom. I'm sure it's because she can afford to be. Not that she's rich. But compared to us, well, she's pretty comfortable.

By Wednesday I not only have some cool new clothes and shoes and things, but Grandma took me to Nordstrom to get a makeover and then bought me makeup. The good stuff. And I actually know how to use it.

On Thursday afternoon, to my surprise, Hilary calls. "Monroe's cousin stopped by and we're going out for ice cream," she tells me. "Want to come along?"

I'm pretty stunned, but I agree. Before they get here to pick me up, I quickly change into a cooler outfit and touch up my makeup.

"Don't you look lovely," Grandma says when I tell her about my plans. "And that's nice that Hilary is introducing you to a boy at your new school."

I try not to show how nervous I am as I watch for a car—what kind of car, I have no idea. I want to ask Grandma if she thinks this is a real date or what. But she's caught up in watching a rerun of *Dancing with the Stars* and I don't want to disturb her, plus I don't want to appear too naive.

Suddenly they're here and I pop out to join them, and the next thing I know I'm sitting in the backseat of Monroe's car—next to a perfectly gorgeous guy. His name is Asher (not Ashton), and although he's polite to me, I can tell he's not comfortable with this situation.

As we wait for the guys to get our ice cream, I discover why.

"Asher has a girlfriend," Hilary tells me.

"Oh." I try not to show my disappointment.

"Yeah, I didn't realize that at first. But he mentioned it on our way to pick you up. He didn't want you to think you were on a date."

"I didn't think it was a date," I say quickly. "Just friends getting ice cream."

Hilary seems relieved. "Oh, good. Apparently his girlfriend's been working at some youth camp for most of August and he's been kind of lonely."

"Right," I say, forcing a casual smile to my lips as the guys rejoin us with the ice cream.

"Just so you know," she says quietly.

"No problem."

I play the good sport as we talk and eat our ice cream, and Asher fills me in about Garfield High and how kids can be kind of snooty there. Then I make this really lame excuse about needing to get home early, and just like that it's over with. Big deal. Yet I feel deflated as I go back into Grandma's house. I flop myself onto her sofa as she sits in her recliner with Millie, watching an old Turner Classic movie, which is a black-and-white musical that's pretty lame.

As I sit there watching a pair of young lovers singing to each other in the garden, I wonder when I'll have my turn—when will I ever get to go out on a real date? If that somehow miraculously happens, will it be with a guy as cool as Asher Gordon? Or someone more nerdy, like his cousin Monroe? And will I ever get my first kiss?

Good grief, my birthday is less than three weeks away now and it seems more than likely that I'll totally nail this one—I'll be that pathetic girl who really did hit sweet sixteen without being kissed.

3

It's Labor Day weekend, but as usual, my mom has to work. To make matters worse, Stacie is still in a snit because I abandoned her last week. And it doesn't help that I got a bunch of new clothes. I thought she was going to punch me in the nose when I let that little cat out of the bag.

"You're so lucky," she says to me as we sit by the pool together on Sunday. I've been working hard to win her favor back, and I'm not even sure it's worth the effort.

"I'm lucky?" I repeat. "I get to start a new school where I know only one person and—"

"Two," she points out. "Don't forget your big date with Asher Gordon." She slams the peach smoothie I made for her onto the cement so hard that I'm worried the plastic cup might crack.

"I told you," I say, "that wasn't a date. Asher already has—"

25

"I know," she says in a snooty voice. "Everyone knows. Asher has been going with Brianna for ages. But that doesn't mean they might not break up. I mean if Asher is into you. And then you'll probably just forget you ever knew me because you'll be Miss Popularity."

"That's so not going to happen," I tell her as I finish the last of my peach smoothie.

"Sure, you can say what you like, but—"

"I have an idea," I say as I suddenly jump to my feet.

She frowns up at me. "What?"

I reach down and grab her hand. "Come on."

"What?" she whines as I pull her up.

"A makeover. We'll give you a back-to-school makeover."

She tries to look skeptical, but I can tell I've got her interested.

"How are you going to do that?"

"You'll see." I point upstairs. "That is, if you're willing. This is a onetime offer that expires in ten seconds."

"Okay, I'm in."

Before she can rethink this agreement, I dash upstairs, and I can hear her trudging up the steps behind me. Of course, I'm not totally sure how I'll pull this magical makeover off. But I suddenly feel quite driven. There are two reasons I'm determined to help Stacie improve her appearance: (1) I want her to get over being mad at me, and (2) perhaps more importantly, I want her to look her best since she's the only friend I'll have when I go to school on Tuesday.

First I make Stacie take a shower and wash and thoroughly condition her hair. If I had a spare toothbrush, I'd force her to brush her teeth. But maybe I can make her run home to do that when we're done. The conditioner alone is a great help to her hair. As I show her how to blow it dry, removing the kinky waves, it's actually rather shiny and pretty. "Now, is there any reason you can't do this for yourself?" I ask her.

She shrugs. "I never knew how."

"Didn't your mom or sister ever—"

"They think I'm hopeless," she admits. "They call me Baby Pig sometimes."

"That's harsh."

She nods sadly. "Leslie tells me that my nose is too big for my face and that my skin will never clear up unless I quit drinking soda, which is not even possible. She says that if I keep going outside with no sunscreen, I'm going to look like I'm eighty by the time I'm twenty. And she says my hair looks like a witch's broom."

"Well, how about if we trim your hair a little," I suggest as I show her how uneven the ends are.

"Do you know how to do that?"

I hold out my long hair as a sample. "I cut my own hair, which is why you don't see any split ends."

She nods eagerly now. "Sure, go ahead."

I trim her hair and the use the curling iron to turn the ends under. But instead of letting her look at it in the mirror, I make her look at me as I decide what to do for her face. "You know, your complexion isn't really that bad," I tell her.

She just laughs.

"I actually think a little foundation and concealer, combined with better skin care, could make a big difference."

"Go for it," she says in an unconvinced tone. So I do.

Now, I've been told that an only child tends to be more selfish than one with siblings, and I think I can attest to the truth in that statement. For that reason, as I continue with the facial portion of this Stacie makeover, I don't use the nice new products that Grandma bought me at Nordstrom. No, for Stacie, I use my old stuff—relatively cheap drugstore items that Mom let me buy after I turned fifteen and was finally allowed to wear makeup. I'm guessing that Stacie won't know the difference.

But I do take time and care to do my best. I even explain to her what I'm doing so she can do it herself at home. "This concealer is to cover blemishes," I say, pretending I'm the gorgeous redhead that worked me over at Nordstrom last week. "Go lightly with it so it's not obvious you're trying to cover something up. Then dab it with your finger a bit to soften the edges. And when you apply the foundation, keep it light too, and make sure you blend the edges along your jaw so there's not a distinct line there." Then I teach her how to use blush. "Just a bit in the apple of your cheek and then feather it out toward your ears so you don't look like a clown."

It seems the only products she actually knows how to use

are mascara and lip gloss. "I swiped the mascara from Leslie," she admits after I've finally managed to remove the clumps from her lashes. "It's waterproof, so I can swim and everything, and I only have to put it on every few days."

"And you never take the old mascara off?"

"It's too hard to get it off."

"Tell me about it." I toss the last blackened tissue away. "Why don't you throw that waterproof junk away and stick to this kind? It might not hold up in a swimming pool, but it does come off nicely at the end of the day."

Next I show her how to put on eyeliner and how to soften it with a Q-tip so it doesn't look like Cleopatra. "Voila," I say when I'm done. "Vive la différence!"

And what a difference there is. When she looks at herself in the mirror, she's as astonished as I am. "Wow, Elise," she says to me. "You're really good at this, aren't you?"

I kind of shrug.

"How did you learn this anyway?"

"I don't know," I admit. "But I do like art, and makeup is kind of like art. Last year when I took drama, I offered to do makeup to escape being cast in the play."

She's smiling now, which actually makes her look even prettier. Then she turns and hugs me. "You might look a lot like my big sister, but you are way nicer."

Well, that really touches me, so I decide to take my unexpected generosity to the next level. "Now, how about clothes?"

"Clothes?" She just frowns. "My, uh, wardrobe isn't exactly—"

"No, I mean maybe I have some clothes that might—"

"Uh, if you haven't noticed, we're not exactly the same size. I mean you're like three inches taller and way more curvy and—"

"But I haven't always looked like this," I remind her. "And I happen to be one of those people who has a hard time letting go of things—even when those things are too small."

"Seriously?"

I go to the back of my closet and retrieve some of my old favorites—some that I saved and bought myself, others that I talked Mom or Grandma into getting. But I have a nice little collection—with the emphasis on "little."

"Wow, you really did used to be smaller." Stacie grins as she zips a pair of what used to be my favorite jeans. "Lucky me!"

"No, *Lucky* jeans. Those are real Lucky's, you know."

"No way!"

I nod and try not to feel envious as I remember how great I used to feel in those jeans. I mean it's not like they'll ever fit me again anyway.

"Are you really okay with this?" she asks hesitantly.

I force a smile. "Well, I guess I kind of wish I could still squeeze into them."

She looks shocked. "You're crazy, Elise. I would totally kill to have your body."

"Just wait, you probably will someday."

"Kill for your body?"

I laugh. "No, I mean you'll probably get your own body—curves and all."

"I told my mom that I wanted a boob job for my next birthday."

Now this makes me really laugh. "And what did she say?"

Stacie rolls her eyes. "She said in my dreams."

It seems that Stacie's dreams have come true today. Or nearly. She's still stuck with no curves. But by the time she leaves my apartment, looking better than ever and loaded down with two grocery bags of used clothes and one plastic bag of old makeup, she's grinning like she just won the lottery.

"You know, Elise," she says as she pauses by the door, "you're the best friend I've ever had. Honestly. When I first met you, I thought you were going to be a stuck-up snob. But you're not. You're totally cool."

"Thanks," I tell her. But even as I say this, I feel a little guilty. The truth is that although I totally enjoyed the process, my original motives about doing this makeover weren't exactly pure. Not that I'll tell her that. It wouldn't make either one of us feel any better.

"I have to go with my mom and sister to a family picnic thing tomorrow," she says, "but maybe we could go to school together on Tuesday . . . I mean if you want. I usually just ride the bus since my mom never gets up on time." She frowns. "The bus otherwise known as the dork mobile."

"My mom's going to drop me off," I tell her. "Why don't you just ride with me?"

Her eyes light up. "Sure, that'd be cool. And maybe my mom could pick us up afterward." She thanks me again and leaves.

On Labor Day morning, Grandma pops in unexpectedly and asks me to drive her over to her sister's house, which is like two hours from here. "Your mom said you were just home alone anyway," she tells me. "And I'm worried that I need to get my eyes checked. I'm just not seeing as good as I used to when I was younger."

So I agree to drive her to Great Aunt Louise's. I suppose it's better than just sitting around freaking over what my new school will be like and wondering if Asher Gordon will even give me the time of day. We end up staying there until evening, which means I'm driving home in the dark, but Grandma insists, assuring me that those hours will look good on my driver's log when I go for my license.

Back at the apartment, I get worried. "How are you going to drive yourself home now?" I ask her. "What about your eyesight?"

She just smiles. "Oh, my night vision is excellent, sweetie," she says as she takes the keys from me. "No problems there."

I have to laugh as I go inside. What a nutty lady. But I

think maybe I can see through her little scheme. She probably knew I'd spend the whole day obsessing about tomorrow. I'll bet she just wanted to give me a little distraction. Really, I appreciate it.

"Are you all ready for the big day tomorrow?" Mom asks as I'm brushing my teeth. We've shared the same bathroom for so many years, I can't even imagine having one to myself, although I think it would be nice to have a little more privacy sometimes. Like now.

"I guess," I say, then spit.

"Picked out what you're going to wear yet?"

"I have it narrowed down to three outfits."

"No matter what you wear, I'm sure you'll look great."

"I know what you're doing, Mom. Trust me, it's not helping."

"What?" She holds up her hands and gives me an innocent look.

"Trying to make this thing seem all peachy keen and wonderful only makes me feel worse, okay?"

She just laughs. "You're going to do fine, Elise. You're a very pretty girl. You're smart and a hard worker. You're talented in so many areas I can hardly keep track. Really, how could it not go well for you?"

While I can think of 1,001 ways how it could go totally sideways for me, I decide not to list them for her. Not tonight anyway. Instead, I kiss her on the cheek, tell her good night, and go into my room. For no particular reason, I open my laptop, my Christmas present from Grandpa before he died last January. I power it up and then go online to check my email, which is completely ridiculous. Who would've sent me something is a total mystery, since the only emails I get anymore are from Grandma "just checking in," or Mom sending me a message from work, but I go through the motions just the same. As usual, there's just a couple pieces of spam, so just as quickly as I turned it on, I turn it off and fold the screen down, snapping it closed.

I stand up and sigh loudly. I close my eyes and wish with all my heart that tomorrow will be a good day. Then I take it one step further and do something I haven't done in months—I actually pray. Standing there in the center of my tiny room with tightly clenched fists, I ask God to help me make it through tomorrow, to help me make some friends, and, if it's not too much to ask, to help me find a relatively cool guy so I can get my first kiss before I turn sixteen.

Now why I think God would want to do this is beyond me. But it's what I pray. Then, promising God that I'll pray more frequently (and thinking that if he answers this desperate little prayer, I absolutely will keep this promise), I get into bed and try to force myself to go to sleep.

4

I make it through the ordeal of locating my locker and navigating my way to my first class without too much trouble. Well, other than high blood pressure, although I try to keep a calm expression on my face. Never let them see you sweat. And I try not to be too obvious about the fact that wherever I go, I'm on the lookout for Asher. Not that I'm under the illusion he'll speak to me or even pick me out of the crowd. But I suppose I'm hoping . . . wishing . . . dreaming.

Then in fourth period, which is second-year Spanish, I see him just as I'm about to go into class, and I honestly think my heart skips a beat or two. But I don't let him know. In fact, I act like I don't quite remember him, like he's one of those guys who just looks like everyone else, which is so bogus because he actually looks a lot like Matthew McConaughey.

"Hey, Elise," he says to me with a brilliant smile that's so Matthew. "How's it going?"

I give him a sort of surprised look, then, cocking my head to one side, I say, "Oh, Ashton, right?"

He laughs. "No, it's Asher."

"Oh yeah." I nod as if I'm soaking this in, like I really didn't remember his name. "Are you in this class?"

"Yep. How about you?"

I nod and go inside the classroom, but my knees feel slightly weak as I take a desk on the sidelines. To my total delight, Asher sits next to me and continues to make small talk with me until the teacher, Ms. Sorenson, steps up and begins to take roll.

I'm actually thankful for this break from Asher because I honestly felt like I was getting light-headed, like I might just pass out and fall limp to the floor. And how embarrassing would that be?

As Ms. Sorenson talks to us (in Spanish) about what this year will be like, I focus on breathing and relaxing and probably miss most of what she's said. Then I realize she's telling us to choose language lab partners or to wait for her to assign them, and the next thing I know, Asher is nudging me.

"Want to be partners?" he asks.

"Sure," I say calmly, hoping desperately that I won't faint from shock. As class continues, I begin to wonder if I'm not really still at home in bed—maybe my alarm didn't go off and I'm late for school, and I'm actually dreaming this whole thing. Just to be sure, I pinch myself. No, this is for real. *For real.*

I am so thankful I started Spanish in middle school, because right now it feels like most of my brain has turned to mush. Fortunately, there's a small part that just goes into some kind of autopilot, and I manage to make it through the class without embarrassing myself.

"You're really good," Asher tells me when class ends. He grins. "I had a feeling you'd be a good partner."

I just thank him and stand up, hoping that I can walk out of here without tripping and falling on my face.

"So do you know anyone yet?" he asks as he continues to walk with me down the breezeway. "Got someone to sit with at lunch?"

"No, not really," I say. Okay, I'm not going to admit to this cool senior guy that I've been hanging with a freshman nobody. I just hope I don't run into Stacie and have her step up and say something lame. She's got to know better than to do that.

"Then stick with me and I'll introduce you to some of my friends."

"Thanks." *Keep breathing*, I remind myself as I walk with him toward the cafeteria. *Just keep breathing.*

He leads me toward a table in the center of the noisy room. Already a number of kids are clustering there. They all look curiously at me. Suddenly I think, *Oh no, what if this is a trick? What if something totally humiliating is about to happen? Why am I so gullible?*

But nothing happens. Asher simply introduces me to everyone who's there, and I try really hard to remember their names. There's Chance and Lindsey, who are a couple. Hayward and Bristol appear to be a couple too. And the other names seem to have evaporated.

"Where's Brianna?" Lindsey asks Asher with a slightly suspicious look in her big dark eyes. She's petite and pretty, with short dark hair that frames her face in a pixielike way.

"That's what I was going to ask you," Asher says to her.

"Oh, there she is," Bristol says. Bristol is tall, about my height, and she has this gorgeous red hair that goes halfway down her back. She waves to a girl who's coming toward the table.

"Hey, Brianna," Asher says in a friendly tone as he embraces her and they exchange a kiss. "I want you to meet a new girl. She's a friend of my cousin, just moved here from Renaldo this summer." As he introduces us, I expect her to be suspicious or jealous or to even say something mean or degrading. Instead, she just smiles brightly and shakes my hand.

"Welcome to Garfield," she says. "Home of the wildcats." She curls her hand into a paw and makes a hissing sound then laughs. "But we're really pretty nice. Most of the time."

I laugh too. It occurs to me that this girl could be one of the Olsen twins—Mary Kate or Ashley. Although she's younger, I want to ask her if she's related. Thankfully I do not.

As we walk over to get in the lunch line, I am stunned at two things. First of all, how easy this was, and second, that I'm being included in what appears to be the A-list crowd. It's like a fairy tale. Unbelievable.

I pay attention to what Brianna and Lindsey pick up for their lunch, and trying not to be too obvious, I imitate them. Although I do go for a different dressing on my salad. I follow them back to the table, almost expecting this too-good-to-be-true scene to go up in smoke, but it doesn't. I sit down in the empty spot next to Bristol and try to appear calm and relaxed. Still, there's a ton of pressure here. Don't say too much, but don't be a mouse. Try to fit in, but don't let them see you trying.

I feel like someone's staring at me, and I glance up and spot Stacie watching me from the lunch line. She's with a couple of girls who I assume are her friends. But her expression is a mixture of shock and concern. I simply look away, returning my focus to opening the stubborn salad dressing packet.

"It must've been hard to switch schools," Bristol says to me. "Leaving all your friends behind. I'd freak if my parents did something like that to me."

"It's been a challenge," I admit as I fork my salad.

"So what are you into?" Lindsey asks.

"Into?" I echo in a lame way.

"You know. Like Brianna and I are cheerleaders. Bristol is into drama. The guys are pretty much jocks." She laughs like that's funny. "What about you?"

"Elise is really good in Spanish," Asher says quickly. "And I was lucky to snag her as my lab partner."

Lindsey glances quickly at Brianna, like she's wondering what her friend will say or do. But Brianna just smiles. "I

39

hated Spanish," she tells me. "I switched to French in my sophomore year."

Then the subject changes to football. From what I can tell, both Hayward and Chance play, but Asher decided to quit this year. And no one is too pleased about it.

"Hey, sorry that I'd like to graduate from high school without being permanently crippled," he tells them, "or suffering another concussion." He looks at me like I should understand and take his side. "I played quarterback and took so many hits last year that my parents got worried I was going to suffer brain damage."

"I think you made the right choice," I tell him, then instantly wish I hadn't said anything.

He grins. "Me too. Maybe I'll go out for basketball. I kind of gave that up for football."

"Well, it just won't be the same this year," Brianna says with a pouty expression. "Cheering for football with my boyfriend sitting in the stands." She shakes her head. "Pretty pathetic."

"You'd rather have a boyfriend who's turned into a vegetable?" I say.

Brianna laughs and pats his cheek. "But you'd make such a cute vegetable. I'd call you Mr. Potato Head."

He chuckles. "Thanks a lot. But if you don't mind, I'd like to hold on to what brains I have left."

They banter back and forth and I realize that I'm mostly just sitting and listening. Maybe I'm like Miss Potato Head. Finally the bell rings, and I'm actually relieved to go to class.

Despite the rush of exhilaration that comes with hanging with the cool crowd, it's also very exhausting. But I have Art next, so it should be kind of like taking a break.

I'm surprised to discover that Bristol is also in Art. And even more surprised when she invites me to sit with her. There are four to a table, and the other two seats are occupied with a lanky-looking guy with dark-rimmed glasses and a pale-faced girl with shoulder-length, mousy hair.

"I'm Phillip Martingale," the guy tells me with a confident smile. His brown hair is on the longish side, and he's actually pretty good looking.

"I'm Elise Storton," I say.

"Elise just moved here from Renaldo," Bristol tells him. "She was friends with Asher's cousin, so Asher's been helping her to meet people."

He nods. "That's cool. So what do you think of old GHS?"

"It seems okay."

Phillip gestures to the quiet girl next to him. "This is Katie, and she's a little on the shy side. Right, Katie?"

Her cheeks flush slightly, but she doesn't say anything.

"Anyway, what Katie lacks in chattiness she makes up for in talent," Phillip says. "She's a real artist."

Before long, I can see for myself that Phillip wasn't kidding. Katie is very good.

Mr. Hanson gives us random pages from a magazine to pull ideas from for a pencil sketch. "Just use the photos as inspiration," he tells us. "This is a chance to warm up your pencils, and for me to get to know everyone's skill level. No pressure."

But Katie jumps right in, and I'm totally impressed. "You're really good," I tell her.

She mumbles, "Thanks," but keeps her eyes on her drawing, which is an old pickup and falling-down fence. How she extracted that from her magazine page is a mystery. It takes me a while to decide what my magazine page is inspiring me to draw (since it's an advertisement for Usher perfume), but I finally decide just to draw his hand, which is wrapped around the bare leg of a woman. Once I get going, I realize it's not bad.

"Wow, sexy," Phillip tells me when he sneaks a peek at my drawing.

I just laugh and show him the magazine ad. "Like I had a choice?"

"I don't know," Bristol says. "Usually our drawings represent pieces of ourselves. Art is subjective like that."

I look at her sketch, which is a really great-looking high-heeled shoe with what appear to be rhinestones decorating the toe. But when I look at her magazine photo, it's just an ordinary-looking woman in sneakers. "How'd you get that shoe from that picture?" I ask her.

She laughs. "It's called imagination, Elise."

I can hear the put-down in her voice, and I'm reminded that I really am out of my league here. I wonder how long I can keep up this charade.

Finally the school day comes to an end, and I'm so thankful to have survived. But now I'm faced with a totally new dilemma. Stacie's mom has offered to pick us up today, but I so don't want to be seen with her. Since school is over, it's okay to use electronics, so I turn on my phone and call Stacie's number, hoping that she's turned her phone back on too. When she answers, I tell her that I've got a ride home with someone else.

"You're kidding," she says. "Who?"

"I'll tell you later."

"Well, you better."

I decide to just hang near the computer lab since that's where my last class was, just trying to waste enough time for me to know she's gone. What I do after that is anyone's guess. Maybe I'll just walk home, although that will take more than an hour and my shoes will pay the price.

"What's up?" asks a guy from behind me.

I turn to see Asher grinning at me.

"Oh . . . nothing," I say.

"Are you waiting to use a computer or something?" He glances over to where some computer geeks are gathering for some after-school "fun."

I make a face. "No. Not even close." I kind of shrug now. "Actually, I was trying to figure out how to get home. My mom was supposed to pick—"

"Why don't I give you a ride?"

"Seriously?"

He laughs. "Yeah. Is anything wrong with that?"

"No, of course not. I'd love a ride."

"Come on then," he says as he starts walking. "My car's in the east parking lot."

"Will Brianna mind?" I ask as I walk with him.

"No. She's got her own car and she's got cheerleading practice anyway. She probably won't leave for another couple of hours."

Once we're settled in his car, which is a very cool Honda Accord, I feel like I can almost relax and actually let out a sigh.

"Long day, eh?" he asks as he backs out.

"Oh yeah."

He turns and smiles at me. "It looks like you held up okay."

"Thanks. Hopefully it'll get easier."

"For sure."

"I like your car," I tell him. "It feels like it's pretty new."

He nods. "Yeah. I'd been hoping for something a little zippier, you know, but my parents thought this was a practical car. And the gas mileage is good, so I guess I shouldn't complain. Except that most of my friends have cars that are a whole lot cooler." He laughs. "But that's pretty juvenile, isn't it?"

I laugh too. "Hey, I'd be really glad to have a car this cool." Suddenly I realize that I'm going to have to tell Asher where I live—and that is totally not cool.

"Want to get a coffee or soda or something before I take you home?" he offers.

"Sure," I say, trying not to sound too eager. This might give me time to come up with a plan to avoid telling him that I live in the Tropicana Suites.

He chooses a coffee place, and we both order iced mochas and sit outside, and he tells me about how this year feels different for him. "It's weird not playing football. I mean it was my choice to quit, but it's like I don't know what to do with my time now. It's like I'm out of sync or something."

"I know how you feel."

He nods. "Yeah, I'll bet you do. Starting a new school, well, that's got to be tough."

"Thanks for making it better," I tell him. "I really appreciate it." I confess how scared I was that I wouldn't make any friends or that I'd get picked on. "But it was actually a really good day."

By the time we finish our coffees, I've come up with a plan. I tell him I live in Arbor Estates, which is a pretty nice condominium development a few blocks away from where I really live. "It's just temporary," I say as he drives me over there. "My mom's job transfer happened so quickly, she hasn't had time to buy something in a better neighborhood yet."

Asher drops me off in the parking lot and I thank him again. I pretend to walk toward one of the buildings, taking my time, and when I know he's gone, I slowly turn around and walk on over to the Tropicana.

I'm just heading up the stairs to our apartment when I

hear Stacie calling my name. I realize I'll have to do some backpedaling and apologizing. To my relief, she's totally understanding.

"It's okay," she tells me. "I mean I was kind of jealous at first. I couldn't believe you got swooped into that crowd. But I actually think it's cool. And I'm only a freshman. I couldn't expect you to hang with me and my friends."

I tell her about how Asher drove me home and how we went for coffee and how I think maybe he's slightly into me. "I mean I know he's got a girlfriend, but it's not like they're married, right?"

"Totally."

"And even though she's really sweet, Asher might be tired of her. I mean she's all into cheerleading and he's quit football . . . maybe they're about to go their separate ways." Of course, even as I say this, I'm remembering Jake and Jocelyn and how I was always imagining a similar scenario about them. And I wonder—what is it with me and couples like this? Is there something Freudian going on?

"Wow." Stacie shakes her head. "You and Asher Gordon . . . that would be so amazing. And you'll have to tell me all the details, okay?"

"I will," I promise her. "As long as you don't mind not hanging with me at school, okay?"

So we agree. And even though this makes me feel somewhat shallow, I think it's for the best. Like Stacie said, she's a freshman and I'm a junior—a junior who's hanging with seniors and juniors and finally making my way into a group of pretty cool friends. Or so it seems.

But the truth is there's this nagging little voice in the back of my head saying, *If it seems too good to be true . . . it probably is.*

5

As it turns out, that nagging little voice was right. Oh, the morning of my second day at school goes fairly smoothly. Spanish with Asher is actually pretty fun, and I can tell he genuinely likes me. But it's like everything changes the moment I enter the cafeteria at lunchtime. Again, I'm with Asher. But this time, Brianna makes a beeline for her boyfriend, and totally ignoring me, she grabs onto him and literally drags him away from me. I'm just standing there unsure of what to do next.

I proceed with caution toward the table where I was so warmly welcomed yesterday. But today I'm met with icy stares. No one offers me a seat. Even when I say, "Hey," I'm totally ignored. It's like I'm being frozen out.

Like yesterday, I vaguely wonder if this is all just a dream— more like a nightmare. But I know it's real. I suppose I'm not really that surprised. I don't know why I thought I could squeeze my way into that group. As I get in the lunch line, I wonder why I even tried. Yet it had just seemed to happen so naturally, like I hadn't really tried at all.

Today I get a cheeseburger to go. I take my lunch outside and wander around the courtyard until I find a solitary spot where I sit and eat in silence. I suppose I'm kind of in shock, but I tell myself that this is all for the best. Really, the pressure of hanging with those kids was too much. I should really be relieved and just accept that this is how it's going to be. I might do that . . . except for one thing—I can't stop thinking about Asher.

I eat half of my cheeseburger, which tastes like sawdust, dump the rest of my lunch, and proceed toward the art department. I'm only mildly surprised to see that Katie is already there. Feeling dejected and pathetic, I go and sit next to her.

"That's nice," I tell her as I admire the pickup sketch she's still working on. "I bet someone would pay good money for that and hang it on their wall."

She just nods and continues shading in a dent on the fender.

Soon the others come in, and I try to avoid eye contact with Bristol as I focus on my own project. I'm trying to get Usher's ring just right—using this obsession to block out the pain that's inside me.

"You looked kind of shocked at lunch," Bristol says quietly.

I glance up and realize she's talking to me. I shrug.

"Maybe you didn't know what was going on."

I consider my options. I could just ignore her like she ignored me in the cafeteria. Or I could try to find out what happened. "I guess I don't really know," I confess. "Well, other than the same old same old—girls being mean to girls for no particular reason."

I see Phillip's eyes glint with interest, and suddenly he's watching us. Not that I particularly care. It seems a small thing to be embarrassed here in Art compared to how I felt in the cafeteria.

"Well, you probably aren't aware that you and Asher were spotted yesterday."

"Spotted?" I frown at her. "What do you mean?"

"I mean you two having coffee. You were seen. And when Brianna found out about it, well, let's just say she's not too happy with you. None of us are."

"But he was just giving me—"

"You can paint it any way you like, Elise. But the fact is you were putting the move on Asher and everyone knows it. And that is so low. I mean we all were nice to you. And this is the thanks we get. Kind of pathetic."

I look over at Phillip, and he looks just as surprised as I am. But he smiles at me—almost as if to say he understands. I just sigh and look back down at my drawing, desperately wishing for this day to end.

When the day finally does end, I'm relieved to catch a ride with Stacie and her mom. Even if their old car looks like a wreck and smells like stale fast food, at least I'll be home soon. Stacie presses me for information as I slump in the backseat. But I'm not talking.

Once we're home, she follows me to my apartment, demanding to know what's going on. Knowing it's the only way to get rid of her, I pour out the whole ugly story. And then I cry.

"Oh, Elise," she says with compassion. "I'm so sorry. That's horrible."

"I know." I reach for another tissue and blow my nose. "I don't even know how it happened. I mean I kind of know. But it all came at me so fast. I guess I wasn't thinking."

"I'll bet Asher really did like you too," Stacie says. "But snooty little Brianna probably threw a hissy fit."

"I guess I can't really blame her," I admit. "I mean they were all so nice to me. They treated me like an equal, like a friend. Then it looked like I was trying to steal her boyfriend, and even though I wasn't really . . . I guess maybe I kind of was . . . I mean I sort of hoped that Asher was into me."

"Well, it's not like Brianna owns him. I mean they're not married or anything."

"I know. But it was still wrong for me to go after him."

Stacie's phone rings and it's her mom. She hangs up and frowns. "Mom said I better get home and do my share of the housework or suffer the consequences. And the consequences mean riding the bus home from school tomorrow."

I thank her for listening and promise not to kill myself.

Now I'm alone in the apartment, and I wonder how it's possible to go from being ecstatically happy one day to totally bummed the next. To distract myself, I turn on the TV and just sit there gazing blankly at the screen. Then I go to my room and have another good cry.

Finally I turn on my computer, telling myself that I'm going to do homework. But first I check email and I'm surprised to see that I have a post from an address I don't recognize. I wonder who gasher@google.com might be, and then it hits me. *Gasher* must be *G Asher*—in other words, *Asher Gordon*. I quickly open it and am stunned to see that it really is from Asher. I'm even more stunned—and touched—at what he's written.

```
Hi, Elise. Sorry about what happened today.
I would've talked to you in person, but that
would've gotten us both into more hot water.
As you can guess by now, Brianna is very
possessive. And she wants me to stay away from
you. But I wanted to let you know that's not
how I feel. It's just that, for now, we need
to keep a lid on things. That means avoiding
each other for a while. Are you good with
that? If we act totally disinterested in each
other, I'll have time to figure things out with
Brianna. Thanks for understanding.

Asher
```

I read the email several times before it fully sinks in. Asher really is into me. It's just that he needs to handle this thing with Brianna the right way. That only shows that he's truly a gentleman. But he's into me! I can't wait to write back. But then I think, *No, I should wait.* No need to appear too eager. So far I've played this thing pretty calmly. I think I should keep it up.

I go and fix myself a snack (to make up for the rotten lunch I endured) and then take my time eating it. Finally, an hour has passed and I can't wait another minute. With trembling hands, I begin to write. But then I realize I've written too much . . . said too much . . . so I go back and start over. It takes several tries before I get it just right. I read it again just to be sure.

```
Hi, Asher. Thanks for explaining everything
to me. It was kind of upsetting, especially
since I thought we were friends. But I can
understand why Brianna reacted like that. And
I respect you for handling it the way you are.
I'm totally cool with avoiding you and acting
like there's absolutely nothing between us. In
case you want to talk or text me, my cell phone
number is 555-3972.

Elise
```

I hold my breath and click send. I just sit there and wait, staring at my laptop like I think it's going to sing and dance. I jump up to make sure my cell phone is on and fully charged. Then, to distract myself, I start doing my homework. Finally it's nearly six o'clock and I'm checking email for like the twentieth time. It appears that Asher has written back. With shaking fingers I open it.

Thanks for writing back, Elise. And thanks for
understanding. As far as the cell phone, it's
too risky. Sometimes Brianna borrows my phone
and I wouldn't be surprised if she checks to
see who I've been talking to. Besides that, I
promised my parents I wouldn't text anymore
after a big bill I got last year. So let's
stick to email. Can't wait to see you at
school tomorrow. But if you catch me looking,
just toss me an icy stare, okay? That'll be
my reminder that we're keeping this thing
undercover for now. And, another thing, let's
ask Ms. Sorenson to find us different lab
partners in Spanish. That'll make this more
believable. Missing you already.

Asher

I can't believe it. Two emails in one night. And the second
one sounds even warmer than the first. He's missing me! He
can't wait to see me. This is so cool.

This time when I write back, my hands aren't shaking. But
I do control myself from saying too much. I really want to
do this right.

I get you about the cell phone. Makes sense.
So does switching lab partners. But I'll miss
you. Don't worry, I'll be sure to give you the
cold shoulder if you so much as glance my way
tomorrow. Just remember that it's only an act.
:-) And hopefully it's an act that I won't be
playing for too long.

Elise

The next morning Stacie and I wait for my mom downstairs, and I quickly fill her in on this latest development. Then I swear her to secrecy.

"This is so cool," she says as Mom is coming. "Really exciting!"

As we ride to school, I talk about other things. It's not that I usually keep stuff from my mom, but I'm not sure she'd understand this. She might think I was selling myself short by keeping up this little pretense. But in time I'll tell her.

It's surprisingly fun to walk around school with this kind of secret to hold on to. When I see Asher on my way to Spanish, he immediately forgets everything and smiles at me like always. I just glare at him. Then to add to the drama, I go straight to Ms. Sorenson and request a change in lab partners.

"Is something wrong?" she asks.

"I'm just not comfortable with him," I tell her quietly. "I'd rather be with a girl, if that's okay. I think I'd have more confidence with a girl."

She smiles as if she understands. "I think Tessa Atkins is feeling like that too," she says. "We'll just make a quiet switch."

"Thank you."

Asher looks surprised when Ms. Sorenson announces that she's switched some lab partners. But I know it's just an act. I suppress the urge to giggle as I toss him another icy stare.

I continue to avoid him, but by the end of the day some of the fun has worn off, and I'm wondering how long we'll have to continue this little act. But when I get home, there's a new email from him. That makes up for everything.

```
You did great today, Elise. So far so good.
Brianna seems to be buying into our charade.
But to make it more realistic, I might try to
approach you at school. Then you can just blow
me off like I'm dirt under your feet. That way
everyone will assume we're not into each other
at all. Because in time, I'm going to break up
with Brianna. I just don't want it to look like
I dumped her for you. If that happens, she'll
set her sights on you. You don't want Brianna
and her friends torturing you for the rest of
the year. So we'll just play this out and do it
right. Then we can be together.

Asher
```

I can't help but jump up and down at this news. He really does plan to break up with Brianna—just to be with me. It's like a dream come true. Or a prayer answered. Then I remember how I actually did pray for this to happen, so I pray again. This time I thank God and promise to be more faithful in my prayers, and I even tell him that I'll start looking for a church.

Because Asher is being so honorable in this whole thing, I wonder if perhaps he's a Christian too. Wouldn't that make sense! In fact, I think I'll mention something about this in my next email to him.

Thanks for writing again. And thanks for your
willingness to protect me like this. Some guys
wouldn't be that considerate. I haven't told
you this yet, but I'm a Christian, and although
I'm not perfect, I try to live my life with
Christian values. I was just curious about you.
You seem like a stand-up kind of guy. What's
your religious background?

Don't worry, I'll remember to treat you like
crud if you try to talk to me. Hopefully
someone will witness my hostilities. But I know
it's going to hurt me inside to be mean to you,
Asher. Because you're a great guy.

Elise

It's on Friday, right after lunch, that Asher actually does approach me. But it's in a corner of a hallway where hardly anyone is around to see us. I'm thinking this is going to be a total waste of drama.

"Why are you so mad at me?" he asks quietly. At first I wonder if this is kind of a practice run, but then I notice that Bristol is coming our direction. Of course, she's on her way to Art too. That's when I realize this is a perfect setup since Bristol is one of Brianna's best friends.

"Why are you trying to talk to me?" I shoot back at him. "You know I can't stand you or any of your other stuck-up friends. So just back off, okay? I've had enough already." I turn from him and storm into the art room, where Phillip is standing by the door.

"Wow," he says to me. "You really told him off."

I nod. "He had it coming."

"Really? What did he do?"

"He used me to make Brianna jealous. And now he wants to act like that's no big deal."

Phillip looks slightly confused, but he nods. "I guess that's a little twisted."

"Well, at least Elise has the sense to keep a safe distance," Bristol says to Phillip. "Some girls wouldn't be that smart."

I roll my eyes, but inside I'm smiling. I'm thinking, *Just you wait, we'll see who's smart.*

As usual, Katie is silently working away—this time it's a charcoal sketch. I'm still stuck with pencils because I'm not as advanced as she is. But I like pencils. I feel like I have more control with them.

"That's looking good," Phillip tells me as he stands to stretch his back and neck.

"Thanks." I check out his sketch. The last time I looked, it was simply the palm of an open hand. He used his own hand as a model, and the drawing seemed pretty realistic, with creases and lines and veins and things. But now there's this dark, gaping hole in the center of the palm.

"Is that . . ."

"What?" he asks.

"Is that supposed to be Jesus's hand?"

58

He nods. "But it's not quite right."

I stare at the hand.

"I think maybe I should've drawn the nail going through instead," he says as he studies his drawing.

"Are you a Christian?" I ask quietly.

He smiles. "Yeah. How about you?"

I nod.

"Where do you go to church?"

"Not really anywhere since I moved from Renaldo."

"You should come to my church." He tears off a corner of his drawing paper and writes down the name of his church, where it's located, and his phone number. "Call me if you want a ride." Then the bell rings and it's time to go.

6

Our little game continues throughout the next week. In response to my question about whether or not Asher is a Christian, he tells me he's a Lutheran who's searching. I like that. It's honest and open. What more could I want?

The truth is I do want more. For one thing, I'm getting a little tired of this game, and I sense by his less frequent emails that he's getting bored with it too. That concerns me. But besides that, I want to know when Asher plans to break things off with Brianna. So on Saturday morning, after not hearing from him for two days, I decide to just toss my cards on the table and ask.

```
I don't want to sound pushy, Asher, but I'm
curious about how long you plan to stay with
Brianna. It's been almost two weeks since I
made her mad. It seems like long enough to
me. I really miss you. We had such a great
```

time together. Sometimes I catch you looking
at me and I can tell you miss me too. So how
about it? Or should I just start flirting with
you at school and see what I can stir up?
Just kidding. I won't do that. At least not
yet.

Elise

I must've hit a nerve because I get a quick response from him. And it's just the kind of response I was hoping for.

You're right to question me, Elise. And
I'm going to be honest with you. This is
complicated. For one thing, I still have some
feelings for Brianna. We've been together for
more than a year and it's hard to just toss
that aside. Also, I promised to take Brianna to
homecoming, and I will look like a total jerk
if I dump her right before the dance. She's
already gotten a dress and everything. So just
be patient, okay? In the meantime, know that
I'm fantasizing about you. In fact, I'd love it
if you'd send me a photo. I'll print it out and
hang it in my room. Here's one for you of me at
the beach last summer.

Asher

I download and print out the photo and just stare at Asher in wonder. He is so good looking. With his shirt off and his tan and his abs . . . well, let's just say this guy is hot.

"Whoa," Stacie says when she finds me in my room still staring at Asher's photo. "He's, like, yummy-licious."

I turn the photo over and smile. "Now I need to send a picture of me. The problem is I don't have a really good one."

"Let's take one," she suggests.

I borrow my mom's digital camera, spruce up some, and strike some poses. Stacie seems unimpressed. "You're really pretty, Elise," she says. "But you should wear your bikini or something with a little more zing."

I laugh. "No way." But I do go back to my closet and pull out a sundress. "How about this?"

"Sure. It's better than your T-shirt anyway."

She snaps a few more shots, and eventually we both agree on one where I'm kind of looking back over my shoulder and making what Stacie describes as a "smoky glance." Then I ask her to give me some privacy and make herself scarce, and she actually takes the hint.

I feel a ripple of caution run through me as I sit down to write an email, and I wonder if this is really such a great idea. I mean talk about putting myself out there. But as I gaze at Asher's picture, I'm swept up into that great smile and those clear blue eyes. And just like that, I attach my own photo, checking it once more just to be sure I really want to send it. I think Stacie's right—it is kind of smoky and smoldering, and it should really warm this guy up. Maybe he'll even rethink his date for homecoming.

But after I hit send, I begin to worry. As much as I try to distract myself with other things, I keep returning to my computer, checking my email about a dozen times, each time feeling more and more worried that he hasn't replied. Finally, I decide that my photo was lame and that he is so over me and I am totally pathetic. And I know I'm losing him.

Then I come up with another plan. Sure, it might be a desperate plan, but I just can't give up this easily. I call up Phillip and ask if he still wants to take me to church with him. He sounds happy to accommodate me. Does he suspect that I might simply be using him? I hope not. I tell myself that I'm not—not really—and that I need to go to church, I should go to church, and this is no big deal.

After church on Sunday, Phillip invites me to get some lunch with him and I agree. Why shouldn't I? Oh, I know my main purpose for connecting with him today is so I can casually mention it to Asher via email, and then he might possibly get jealous. I know that's pathetic.

I have to wonder why I can't be attracted to someone like Phillip. Not only is he smart and funny and nice, he actually seems to be into me. Plus his church is pretty cool. Yet all I can think about is Asher.

"See you tomorrow," Phillip says as he drops me off where I really live (the Tropicana Suites). I see no reason to put up pretenses with him.

"Thanks for everything," I say. "I had a great time!" I go into my room and immediately start writing an email.

```
Hi, Asher. I think honesty is key to any good
relationship, so I must be honest with you
and tell you that I was just out with Phillip
Martingale. While he's not you, he's not bad.
In fact, he's actually pretty cool. He's not
tied up with some other girl either. So if you
see me with him at school, don't be surprised.
We can just make it part of our little act.
Unless you're ready to end this act. I really
think I am. In fact, I might simply approach
you tomorrow. I'll act like I'm not mad anymore
and ask if we can just be friends. That seems
believable. Don't you think?

Elise
```

The day slowly passes without a word from Asher. As Mom and I are having dinner together—kind of a rarity in this household—she asks if I'm okay. "You seem worried about something," she says with concerned eyes.

Since I haven't had Stacie around today (her older sister took her shopping), I decide to dump on Mom. Well, not everything. Mostly I just explain how Asher and I have become good friends and how we've been emailing and how he plans to break up with Brianna. "But I'm not so sure now," I say. "It's like things have kind of cooled off between us."

I don't mention my little ploy to make Asher jealous by using Phillip. I'm actually feeling kind of creeped out by that myself. How low will a girl go? Yet I feel desperate. I don't want to lose Asher.

"He sounds like a nice boy," Mom says cautiously, almost as if she wants to say more but is worried she'll shut me down. "And sticking with his girlfriend until he takes her to homecoming is kind of an honorable thing, Elise. You can't really fault him for that. He hasn't known you that long. Maybe he's just trying to figure things out. You should give him more time."

"How much more time?"

Mom smiles in a sad way. "I remember being a teenager. Sometimes one day felt like eternity. Trust me, it'll pass a lot more quickly than you think. Just focus on something else for a while. And don't forget, you have your birthday to look forward to. You still haven't told me what you want."

"You mean besides Asher Gordon?" I sigh.

Mom laughs. "You want me to go out and trap the boy, wrap him up, and set him on our doorstep for you?"

I make a face at her.

"Just be patient, Elise. Remember, good things come to those who wait."

I'm so tempted to point out how that hasn't been the situation with her. She just waits and waits and waits . . . and nothing very good seems to come her way. At least not in the form of romance. But I tell her I have homework, and she says she'll clean the kitchen tonight.

When I turn on my computer, I'm pleased to see that Asher has written. But he's not offering to dump Brianna like I'd hoped. Still, he kind of echoes what Mom just told me.

```
I don't blame you for going out with Phillip,
Elise. He seems like a nice guy. But if you
make a scene with me at school, don't you think
it'll hurt Phillip's feelings? It won't help
things with us much either. You're just going
to have to be patient until after homecoming.
Then things will change. I promise you. Since
I'm willing to wait for you, it seems like
you should be willing to wait for me. I think
you're worth it, Elise. I think about you all
the time. And that photo is great. Although you
have to admit I showed a lot more skin in mine.

Asher
```

I get out his photo and stare at it. Really, I think both Asher and Mom are right. Some things are worth waiting for. I also think it was a cheap shot for me to use Phillip like I did. But then I tell myself that maybe Phillip and I can be friends. I did like his church. So what's wrong with just hanging with him because he's a nice guy and a good friend? Of course, I don't have to tell Asher that. He doesn't need to know everything. Yet I want him to know everything about me. So I decide to just use this time to talk about other things. Why not?

```
I think you're right about not rushing things,
Asher. Sorry to sound so impatient. It's only
because I really like you. Sometimes it's hard
to stand by and just wait. It's like I want to
jump up and grab what I want—take what I think
should be mine. I think you'd be glad if I did.
I think we'd be really good together.
```

I remember when we first met this summer—it's
like we had an instant connection. And when
you put the move on me in Spanish, I could
feel the electricity. I know you could too.
I'll just keep these things close to me, and
I'll wait for you. But please don't make me
wait too long. I might not be able to control
myself.

Elise

This time I don't reread my post before I hit send. I've decided that if this relationship is meant to be, I need to be honest and open with my feelings. Who knows, maybe that will make Asher want to finish things off with Brianna a bit quicker.

To my surprise, I get another email back about half an hour later.

Think about it, Elise, email is a great way
to get to know someone better. So I'll tell
you a secret about me and you can tell me a
secret about you. I'm only telling you this
because I know I can trust you completely.
Here goes. When I was a little kid, I went to
summer camp, and—this isn't easy to say—a camp
counselor kind of messed with me. You know
what I mean? I never told anyone, but it still
bugs me. It feels good to tell you, Elise. I
know I can trust you. Now tell me something
about you so I won't feel like I'm just
hanging here. Okay?

Asher

Wow, I can't believe he just told me this. But I think it's awesome cool that he trusts me like that. I realize this is a great opportunity. We can really get to know each other so when we actually start going out, it'll be like we've been together for a long time already.

```
You know your secret is safe with me, Asher.
I'm totally honored that you'd tell me. It
makes me wish I had something really huge to
tell you. But I will tell you this, and no one
else really knows. I'm going to turn sixteen
next week and I've never been kissed. I think
that's why I'm so impatient to get together
with you. Just imagine how great it's going to
be when we do get together. I can hardly wait.
But I will.

Elise
```

It's pretty late when I hit send, and I realize I'm still not done with homework. I push thoughts of Asher from my mind and focus on my studies until I'm too sleepy to focus on anything.

To my dismay, the emails between us slow down during the next few days. Consequently, I'm slightly fed up. And every time I see Asher and Brianna together, I get even more fed up. That's probably why I spend more time with Phillip. I'm hoping that Asher will understand how he's making me feel. Besides that, Phillip is fun, and he's a good friend. I just hope he's not assuming we're more than friends.

Thursday is my birthday, and when I get up, I decide that no matter what happens with Asher and Brianna today, I will be happy. I put on one of my favorite outfits and take care with my makeup and hair. When I emerge from my room, both my grandma and mom are there to greet me, singing "Happy Birthday."

"Grandma!" I exclaim. "I can't believe you drove all the way over here for my birthday. That is so sweet."

"Happy sweet sixteen," she says as she exchanges glances with Mom. "Actually, I came over to help deliver a surprise that your mom and I have been cooking up these past few months."

"A surprise?" I look at Mom.

Mom hands me a little box, like what jewelry would come in, and says, "Happy birthday, Elise."

I untie the blue ribbon and open the box to see a set of car keys nestled in the cotton. "No way," I whisper, looking from Grandma to Mom and back to Grandma again. They're both nodding and grinning.

"Grandma picked it up at the dealer for me yesterday," Mom tells me.

"I drove it over here this morning," Grandma says.

But I'm already out the door with them trailing behind me, filling in the various details about how they executed their little plan—how Mom has been saving for a year, which explains why money is always tight. I'm just relieved it's not Grandma's old Caddie, although I would be thankful for any kind of wheels. I'm totally shocked and practically speechless when the car turns out to be a light blue Mustang.

"That's it, honey," Mom tells me.

I just stare at her and then the car. This is way too cool. This can't be real.

"Don't you like it?" Grandma asks.

"No way!" I squeal. *"No way!"*

"It's not brand new," Mom explains. "But it's been thoroughly checked, and it seems to be in great condition."

"And low mileage," Grandma says as I open the door and peer inside.

"It's absolutely gorgeous," I tell them. "I love it! I totally adore it!"

Mr. Galloway comes over to check it out. "Wow, that's quite a little car, Elise. If you ever want to loan it out, I'd be glad to—"

"No," Mom says firmly. "One condition is that only Elise is to drive this car."

"Don't worry," I assure her.

"And you have to get your license," Grandma tells me. "That's why I had you doing all that driving for me—so you'd be ready to take your test."

"This is so cool," I say as I hug them both. "Thank you so much!"

"Grandma has offered to take you to the DMV after school today," Mom tells me. "If you think you're ready, that is."

"I'm ready now," I say with confidence. "I'll take the manual to school with me and go over it some more whenever I get the chance."

Now Stacie has joined us, and she's almost as incredulous as I am over this sweet set of wheels.

It's time to head to school, and Grandma offers to get us there if we can take the Mustang. "Hey, I'm fine with that," I say as I hand over my keys. "I just wish it was me behind the wheel."

"You can drive, Elise." She hands me back the keys. "At least until we get to school. Then I'll have to drive it back."

"This is so awesome," I say as I start the engine. I feel like I'm on top of the world as I drive my sweet blue car to school. What a day!

That's when I decide that today is not about Asher and whether or not he's into me. Today is about being sixteen, having a great car, and just plain happiness.

Before Grandma leaves with my car, I take a picture of it on my cell phone. I want to sneak peeks at it throughout the day, and maybe I'll show Phillip too.

7

As usual, I feel awkward and conspicuous when I walk into school. Stacie actually has other girlfriends that seem happy to see her, and I try not to feel envious over my obvious lack of friends. But hey, it's my birthday and I have a great car, so I refuse to let this get to me as I head for the language arts department. On my way I see Phillip, so I go straight for him, open up my phone, and show him the picture of my new car.

"My birthday present," I say proudly. "And if I get my license this afternoon, I'll drive it to school tomorrow."

"Awesome," he tells me. "I'll bet it can really go."

"It's also got low mileage," I say. As we're standing there looking at my cell phone picture and I'm describing how the Mustang's totally loaded, I feel someone watching us. When I glance up, I notice Asher and Chance nearby staring at me. I toss them both a big smile, hold up my phone, and say, "It's my birthday and this is what I got."

They look kind of shocked, probably because I'm actually speaking to them. I hope Asher's not getting all worried that I'm about to blow his cover, but since he hasn't sent me an email in a few days, I'm not sure I even care. Then I see this look in his eyes—kind of a vulnerability or maybe even a longing, or else I'm just imagining things—and I feel guilty for messing with him like this. I just shrug, like I couldn't care less what they think, then turn back to Phillip, and we talk about my car until the first bell rings.

In English Comp, I remember the secrets Asher and I shared . . . and I wonder if that's what made him look like that. Was he freaking that I might tell someone about what happened to him as a kid at summer camp? I so wouldn't. Or maybe he realized that it was my birthday today and that I still haven't been kissed. Maybe he even wished he could kiss me. Or maybe he was worried that Phillip was going to get this opportunity. Not that it's going to happen. No, I've decided I'm going to wait for Asher. He is worth waiting for.

Asher totally surprises me as we're leaving Spanish. He actually smiles at me, tells me happy birthday, and asks to see the photo of my car. I make sure no teachers are looking as I pull out my phone and turn it on. We're not supposed to have phones on during the school day, although most kids break this rule during lunch.

"Wow," Asher says, "that's one nice-looking set of wheels. You wouldn't want to trade with me, would you?"

I laugh. "Yeah, right."

We're still walking together when we get to the cafeteria, and suddenly I'm nervous. "You probably don't want Brianna to see me with you," I say quickly.

"Why not?"

I look curiously at him. "You're not worried?"

He laughs. "Hey, if Brianna wants to pull her jealousy act, let her."

"Seriously?"

But before he can answer, Brianna swoops in from out of nowhere, takes him by the arm, and in a bubbly voice begins telling him about the "funniest thing that happened in Chemistry just now." She totally ignores me, and Asher actually tosses me an apologetic glance, which I'm thinking is a little risky considering not only Brianna but also her friends are watching. But I just smile and give a little finger wave as I get in the lunch line.

Still, as I get my tuna sandwich and soda, I'm thinking this is weird. Asher is acting pretty out of character today. I wonder if this is why I haven't heard from him for a few days—maybe he's been reconsidering his plan. Maybe he's getting ready to break up with Brianna. But homecoming is still a week away, and I can't imagine him dumping her when it's this close. In fact, I'm not even sure I'd want him to.

As I carry my lunch to the cashier, I see Asher watching me again—and he's watching with way too much interest. Not only that, but Brianna's eyes are on him. It's like he's totally oblivious. Now I'm feeling really nervous.

74

"Hey, Elise," Phillip calls out. "Want to eat outside today?"

I smile and nod. "Yeah, it's too sunny to be stuck in here."

I'm relieved to get away from this situation. Not that I wouldn't want to stay with Asher. But not with Brianna acting like that. No, I'm remembering some of the warnings Asher gave me about his possessive girlfriend, and I'm thinking I'd be smart to keep a safe distance.

"I noticed you talking to Asher," Phillip says as we sit at one of the outside tables.

"Yeah, I was kind of surprised he talked to me," I admit.

"You mean considering Brianna."

I nod as I peel the plastic wrap off my sandwich.

"I've known Brianna since grade school." He sticks a straw in his juice bottle.

"Uh-huh?" I take a bite and wait.

"And she's good at looking sweet and innocent on the outside . . ."

"But what about the inside?"

He shakes his head. "I'd just be careful if I were you, Elise."

"Careful?"

"About Asher."

"Why?" Okay, I know the answer, but I have to play like I don't.

"Brianna and Asher have been together for a while, and she's not going to take it lightly if you come between them. You know that."

"So are you saying that Asher has to stay with Brianna just because she might throw a hissy fit if he breaks up with her? Like she's holding him hostage or something?"

Phillip laughs. "It probably sounds like that. But no, that's not what I meant. I'm just saying be careful . . . watch your back."

"Like Brianna might stab me in the back?"

"Not literally. But yeah, she's been known to do some pretty mean things. Sneaky things. And then she kind of glosses over them with that sweet little smile of hers."

I consider this as I take another bite. I wonder why I always seem to fall for the guy with the mean girlfriend. Okay, not always. This is only the second time. But I ask myself again, why can't I crush on someone like Phillip?

I glance at him. He's attractive. He's nice. He's even a Christian. Why am I so obsessed with Asher instead of Phillip? Is it simply because I want what I can't have?

"So how's your birthday going so far?" Phillip asks as we're finishing our lunch.

I smile at him. "It's pretty great. Now if I can just pass the driver's test for my license, I think I would be perfectly happy." I reach into my bag and extract the dog-eared DMV manual. "I guess I should be studying now."

"Want me to quiz you on some things?" he asks.

"Cool." I hand over the booklet, and we sit there in the sunshine as he tests my knowledge. For the most part, I pass.

"I think you're going to do fine," he tells me as he hands back the manual.

"I hope so." I stand and gather up my lunch debris to toss in the trash. Phillip does the same. Then he looks at me and grins. "Let me guess."

"Huh?" I look at him. "What?"

"You're sweet sixteen, but I'm guessing you've already been kissed."

I laugh nervously.

Then, to my shock and disbelief, he puts both hands on my cheeks and pulls my face toward him. I think, *Oh no, he's going to kiss me.* But he leans down and simply kisses my forehead.

"Just in case," he says lightly. We both laugh and head toward the art department together.

I think Phillip is a really good friend. I just hope he's not wanting more than that.

I consider his warning as I work on a pen-and-ink drawing in class. There are a couple of times when I see Bristol watching me with narrowed eyes, like maybe she's warning me to back off too. I wonder if Brianna asked her to spy on me. Or maybe I'm just being totally paranoid. Whatever the case, I plan to email Asher and demand to know what's going on. Why has he told me to be so secretive about our relationship and then suddenly he's, like, totally in my face?

Finally my last class ends. I hurry out to the passenger pickup area, spot my adorable blue Mustang, and jog over to it. It's all I can do not to bend over and hug this sweet ride. Instead, I climb into the passenger seat and open up my DMV manual.

"You all ready for the test?" Grandma asks as she pulls out into the street.

"I think so." But as I skim over the words, I shoot up a silent prayer, begging God to help me with the test. Once we're there, I feel surprisingly calm as I take the computer part of the test, but then I get nervous as I wait for the results. To my relief, I pass. Then it's on to the actual driving test.

Grandma gives me a thumbs-up and a grin. "Go get 'em, Elise."

The DMV guy is pretty serious and grim as I start the car. I tell him it's my birthday, and he tells me to focus on my driving. So I do. And I actually do pretty well.

"I marked your score down for having your front tires on the line at the crosswalk," he tells me. "Watch out for that."

"But did I pass?" I ask.

He actually smiles. "Happy birthday."

I control myself from jumping up and down as I thank him. I go get in line to have my picture taken, grinning as the woman snaps a shot.

"I think we should go out and celebrate," Grandma tells me when I show her the small plastic card. "How about ice cream?"

So we go to the ice cream shop and get hot fudge sundaes, then I drive her all the way back to Renaldo.

"You're sure you're okay to drive back on your own?" she asks. "Because this will be your first time driving alone. You won't be too nervous, will you?"

I just grin. "I can't wait."

"Now remember, no cell phone," she warns me. "And be careful."

I promise her I will, then I slowly pull out and drive down the street. Her words, "Be careful," echo in my head, and I remember how Phillip said the same thing earlier today. Except he was talking about Brianna.

I make it home without any problem. I park my car in the numbered space for our apartment, and as I'm on my way upstairs, I'm met by Stacie. "Did you pass?" she asks.

I nod and grin.

"Will you take me for a ride?"

"Maybe a quick one," I tell her as we stand midway on the stairs. "But let me use the bathroom first. And I want to be back before my mom gets home."

She hands me a card. "Happy birthday!"

I thank her and open it to find she's written something sweet inside. "So far this has been a really good day," I say as I continue up the stairs.

"There's a surprise for you at your door too," she tells me.

"Wow!" I exclaim when I see a bouquet of red roses. "Who sent these?"

She giggles. "Who do you think?"

"I don't know." I turn to peer at her. "Not you, right?"

She laughs. "Like I can afford sixteen long-stemmed red roses."

"Did you see who brought them?"

"You mean the florist van?"

"Oh." I reach for the card. "Maybe my mom."

"Or maybe Asher," she says in a seductive-sounding voice. "Hurry, open it, I can't stand the suspense."

"It was Asher!" I exclaim as I silently read the card. *Happy sweet sixteen, Elise. Love, Asher.* He actually wrote, "Love, Asher." What does this mean?

"This is so romantic," Stacie gushes. "I want your life. You get a great car. The coolest guy in school sends you red roses, and you know what that means, right? Red roses are the symbol of love. Elise, you're so lucky you make me sick!" But she's smiling as she says this.

"But how could Asher possibly know where I live?"

"Why wouldn't he?"

"Because as far as he knows, I live in Arbor Estates." I study the card closely, trying to remember what his handwriting looks like. Then I realize he could've called in the order, and the florist might've written this.

"Maybe he got your address at school," Stacie tells me. "You know Bristol is an office assistant. She could've gotten it for him."

"But wouldn't Bristol tell Brianna?"

"Oh, why ask so many questions, Elise? Just enjoy the roses. Man, if I were in your shoes, I'd be dancing!"

"Yeah," I tell her. "You're right." I unlock the door, and with my roses in my arms, I dance into our apartment. I set the roses on the tiny kitchen table and then dance into the bathroom.

"Hey, I want to check my email before we go," I tell Stacie after I come out. "It'll just take a minute."

She follows me into my bedroom and waits as I turn on my laptop. Sure enough, there's a post from Asher. I quickly open it.

```
Happy birthday, Elise! I hope you got my gift
by now. Sorry for getting carried away today,
but you looked so hot, I couldn't keep my
eyes off you. Even so, I have to stick to my
commitment. I can't break up with Brianna until
AFTER homecoming. You've got to help me with
that, Elise. It won't be easy.

Right now I'm just staring at your photo and
wishing you were here with me. In fact, can you
send me some more photos? Please? It will help
get me through this next week. And this time,
please, please, send me something really sexy.
Show a little more skin. Like a swimsuit shot.
Or maybe something even more. Because you are
so hot, babe. I can't wait until we're going
out and everyone knows it.

Love, Asher
```

"Oh my gosh!" Stacie exclaims.

"Did you read that?" I demand.

"Uh, yeah, sorry. Was I not supposed to?"

"There is such a thing as privacy."

"Wow, Asher is totally in love with you, Elise."

I exit my email and snap my computer shut.

"You're going to send him more photos, aren't you?"

"I don't know."

"Come on," she urges. "Asher is practically begging you."

"Let's go for our ride," I say quickly.

"But you should send him another photo," she persists. "I mean look at those roses. Read his email again. The guy is nuts in love with you. He's like over the moon. Come on, Elise. At least a swimsuit shot. He sent you one. And you look fantastic in a swimsuit."

I roll my eyes.

"Come on," she says. "I'll take it for you."

"What about a ride in my car?"

"You can give me a ride to school tomorrow. This is more important."

"I don't know . . ." I frown.

"Just get your swimsuit on," she tells me.

She finally wears me down, and I put my swimsuit on and get Mom's camera again, posing as Stacie shoots. "Make that sultry look again." She coaches me like she's a photographer for the swimsuit issue of *Sports Illustrated*. "Come on, Elise, work with me."

I giggle and strike some more poses until finally I tell her, "Enough!" I dash to the bathroom to get dressed, and by the time I'm back, she's downloading the pictures onto my computer and browsing through them.

"You could probably be a model," she says as she opens

another photo and shakes her head. "Seriously, have you ever considered it?"

I just laugh. We finally settle on a pose of me sitting on the bed with one leg crossed over the other. My knee is up high and I've got my elbow on it, with my chin resting on my fist, and I'm making a sassy little smile. It's actually pretty funny.

"Okay," I tell Stacie. "If I'm going to send this, I'd like a little privacy to write Asher a note. Do you mind?"

Stacie makes a face. "Sometimes you act just like Leslie."

"Then scram, little sister," I tease.

After she's gone and my door is closed, I reread Asher's email. I have to agree with Stacie, the boy's got it bad for me. That is so cool!

```
Thank you for the roses! They are so beautiful.
I'm curious how you got my real address,
though. I'm relieved too. I should've just told
you the truth in the first place, but I wanted
to impress you. We aren't rich. But at least
I have a cool car, huh? Anyway, here is your
photo. I hope it will keep you happy for the
next week. And then we'll be together.

Love, Elise
```

Just as I hit send, Mom gets home and is calling out to me. I tell her the good news about getting my license, and she oohs and ahhs over my roses. Then she takes me out to dinner. Italian. All in all, it's a perfect day.

8

I can't believe how cool it feels to drive my own car to school on Friday. I'm very careful, and I keep my cell phone turned off. I even tell Stacie she has to be quiet so she doesn't distract me. Then I park slightly away from the other cars. I don't want someone opening the door and smacking Bonnie Blue. Yes, I named my car. I've always loved *Gone with the Wind*, and Bonnie Blue is Scarlett's little girl. Unfortunately, Bonnie Blue dies, but this Bonnie Blue is alive and well. Okay, she's as alive as a car can be.

I pat the car on the hood. "Be good, Bonnie Blue," I say, and Stacie laughs so loudly that she snorts.

"Maybe you should cover her with a blankie," she teases.

"Maybe so."

Today I'm going to be on my best behavior, I've already decided. I will not smile or flirt or anything with Asher. In fact, I will simply give him the cold shoulder like I've been doing in the past. Later he'll thank me for it.

It's not easy since I keep getting the feeling he wants to talk to me. I try to send him subtle clues with my eyes. But he isn't getting it. I think Stacie is right, the guy is totally in love with me. I can't help but feel powerful as I continue to chill him out. This is so not like my life.

Finally the day ends, and Phillip walks me out to the parking lot to get a glimpse of Bonnie Blue. Stacie and a friend are staying after school to try out for a part in *No, No, Nanette*.

"Wow." Phillip runs his hand over the shiny rooftop. "Sweet."

I'm all smiles. "I know. I can still hardly believe it myself."

"I'll bet she can really go too."

"Not that I'll be testing that out anytime soon—or ever," I say. "No way will I take any chances with this baby."

"Do I get a ride?" Phillip asks hopefully.

"Sure," I tell him. "Just promise not to distract me. My mom wasn't too sure about me giving rides to anyone. She thinks our state should change the law so that minors aren't allowed to transport minors. But I promised her I'd be really careful."

He holds up his hand like he's making a pledge. "I solemnly swear not to distract you in any way, shape, or form."

I'm just unlocking the door when I notice Asher coming my way. "Is that your new car?" he calls out.

Now I don't know what to do. I try to send him a signal with my eyes because there are a lot of students still hanging in the parking lot. Maybe not Brianna or her friends, but he's got to know that someone is going to see him talking to me. Someone will relay this news back to Brianna. Why risk it now?

"Hey, this is nice." Asher casually comes over like it's the most natural thing in the world. "Lucky girl." He eyes Phillip. "You guys going for a little joy ride?"

"Not a joy ride," I say in a chilly voice.

"I talked her into taking me for a spin," Phillip says lightly.

"I'd like to take a spin too." Asher smiles at me. "But maybe another time."

"Or not," I say in a flippant tone. As in, *What are you doing?* I wonder if he's gotten my latest email with the swimsuit photo. Just the thought of that makes me blush. Maybe it wasn't such a good idea. I can't believe I let a fourteen-year-old talk me into something like that. It's so middle school.

Asher frowns at me, almost like he's hurt or maybe even angry that I'm with Phillip. But I suspect it's just an act. At least he seems to be remembering our plan.

"Well, be careful," he warns me. "A car like that can probably get a girl into some serious trouble."

I just laugh and shake my head as I get into the car. But I'm relieved to get away from him. How am I supposed to keep up my side of this drama if he keeps breaking the rules? *What is wrong with that boy?*

"I think he's into you," Phillip says.

I toss a worried glance his way. Did I actually just say that out loud?

"Seriously, Elise. I think Asher is crushing on you."

I wave my hand then slip the key into the ignition. "You're imagining things. Now don't forget you swore not to distract me."

He nods and looks straight ahead. "Right."

But I do feel distracted as I drive away. I can feel Asher watching us—and that gives me a mixture of pleasure and fear. I'm thinking there is no way he's going to make it through one more week of pretending to still be with Brianna. Really, what's the point?

After dropping Phillip back at school, I drive home and go straight to my computer, hoping that Asher's written. But he hasn't. That worries me, so I decide to initiate this particular communication myself.

```
Asher, you have no idea how rattled you made
me feel in the parking lot this afternoon.
Everything in me wanted to respond to you. And
I would've loved to have taken you for a ride.
But what about our plan? You can't go around
acting this way if you want to keep this thing
under wraps. Even Phillip mentioned that he
thinks you're crushing on me. Now I'm wondering
if you've changed your mind. Maybe you do
want to break up with Brianna after all. If
that's how you really feel, why not just get
it over with? Maybe she'll have time to round
up another guy to take her to the homecoming
dance. Really, it seems kind of unfair to lead
```

```
her along like this. Why not just tell her
you're finished?

Love, Elise
```

As I hit send, I feel a rush of hope. Maybe this really will be it. Maybe Asher will finally cut that girl loose.

But by the time I'm getting ready for bed on Friday—another Friday night spent at home because I didn't want to risk throwing all my cards on the table if I ran into him at the football game—I still haven't heard back. Now I'm worried that maybe he's going to cut *me* loose. Maybe I've been too pushy. Maybe I'm making him realize that he wants to stay with Brianna.

Saturday comes and still no email. But at least Phillip calls. He invites me to church again, offering me a ride. I remind him that I have my own car now, and he acts disappointed. So I offer him a ride instead, and he accepts.

"Come to church with me tomorrow," I urge Stacie on Saturday night. I think that if I have Stacie with me, it won't seem like Phillip and I are there as a couple. As silly as this sounds and as unlikely as it is that he'll ever find out, I feel worried that Asher might not like me spending too much time with Phillip. But Stacie refuses.

While church is good, I feel distracted by two guy problems. First, I still haven't heard back from Asher. And second, I suspect Phillip is more into me than I am into him. He proves this when I drop him off at his house.

"Why don't you go to the homecoming dance with me?" he asks in an offhand kind of way. "It might be fun."

"Oh, I don't know . . ."

"We don't have to be boyfriend-girlfriend to go," he says. "We can just go as friends."

I promise him that I'll think about it. The more I do, the more I think maybe it's not such a bad idea. In fact, if Asher is still with Brianna by then, which I'm guessing he might be, at least I can see him . . . and maybe I can figure out if he's stringing me along or what.

By Sunday afternoon, I receive another email from Asher. Of course, he says all the right things. All the right things and a whole lot more. I'm literally tingling after I read and reread it a few times. But I try to act normal since Stacie is here. She came by to borrow a belt and now I can't seem to get her to leave.

I decide to read his email once more, taking my time as Stacie continues perusing my closet like it's her mini Macy's.

> Elise! Thank you, thank you for the photo! I love it. And I love you! But I just can't get enough of you.
>
> This is going to be the longest week of my life. I even hinted to Brianna that maybe we should break up, but she threw such a fit about homecoming that I was worried for your sake. Please send me more photos. You are so

```
beautiful. So much sexier than Brianna. But
besides that, you're a really nice girl. I love
that you've never been kissed. I can't wait to
be the first one. There's so much I can't wait
for. Thank you for being patient.

Now send me more photos, please! And don't be
afraid to show more skin. You are gorgeous,
babe! And I want more!!!

Love, Asher
```

"You're not going to tell me what he said?" Stacie asks me for like the fifth time.

"No," I tell her. She's been here for about an hour now, and I'm really wishing she'd go home. Not that I don't like her, but I'd like to write back to Asher in private.

"Just a teeny little hint?"

"Okay. But then you have to leave because I have homework."

She rolls her eyes. "Yeah, right."

"He said a lot of nice things," I tell her as I scan his words again. "And he really wants to break up with Brianna, but he's going to wait until after homecoming—"

"Does that mean you'll go to homecoming with Phillip?"

"Maybe."

"What else? Come on, did he like the swimsuit photo?"

I nod and grin. "Yeah. He liked it a lot."

"I knew he would. It was really good. I'm thinking maybe I should become a photographer."

"Yeah, whatever."

"And . . . ?"

"And, naturally, he wants me to send more photos. Of course, being that he's a guy, he wants me to send ones showing even more skin." I giggle nervously. "Not that I plan to."

"Why not?"

"Because it's stupid and skanky and slutty, that's why."

"But girls do it all the time."

"Not this girl."

"Oh, don't be such a prude, Elise. Think about it. Maybe that's what it'll take to get him to break up with stupid Brianna."

"I still wouldn't do it."

"Even if it meant that you'd have Asher Gordon all to yourself? No more Brianna?"

"Not like that," I tell her.

"I don't see what the big deal is, Elise."

"The big deal is that it's skanky. And I'm not that kind of a girl, okay?"

She makes a face. "Okay. But I hope you're not blowing this."

I fake a laugh then turn my back to her, taking my laptop into a corner of my room, where I can hopefully have some privacy since it doesn't look like Stacie plans to leave anytime soon. I hope I'm not blowing it as I quickly type out my response. I basically tell Asher thanks for the compliment, but nice girls don't send nude photos to anyone—period. End of conversation.

Stacie is still going through my closet, complaining that my wardrobe is so much better than hers. Meanwhile I'm sitting here stewing. I mean, as much as I like Asher, I'm a little put out that he asked something like that of me. I'm halfway tempted to write him another email and tell him I'm done with him. But suddenly there's another email from him, and feeling hopeful that he's realized he was wrong to ask this of me, I open it.

```
I thought you loved me, Elise. But I guess
I was wrong. I've trusted you with something
really personal—remember what happened to me
at camp? And now you treat me like this. I'd
be lying if I pretended this doesn't hurt. I
want our relationship to be built on trust. But
I can see you don't trust me. Maybe you never
did. I'm sorry I trusted you now. I guess I
just thought you were someone else. I won't
bother you again. Please don't write back if
you can't trust me.

Asher
```

I don't know how to react to this email. Is he really trying to end this thing? Just because I wouldn't send that photo?

"What's wrong?" Stacie asks.

I decide to just ignore her.

"I can tell something's wrong," she says. "What is it?"

"Nothing." I close my computer and sigh.

"Come on, just tell me, Elise." She really is starting to remind me of a pesky little sister.

I give her a blank look.

"You're, like, totally bummed. I can tell. What's wrong? You can talk to me."

"Okay . . . The problem is that Asher is really hurt because I refused to send the photo."

"You already told him you wouldn't send it?"

I just nod.

"Of course he's hurt. He probably thinks you don't like him."

"I don't think we'll be emailing anymore."

"That's so wrong."

"I guess it makes me sad too." I feel a lump growing in my throat when I think that this relationship—this relationship that never really started—is actually going to end.

"It should make you sad," she says. "It makes me sad too. You guys would've made such a great couple."

"I know it's because of me . . ."

"Well, of course it's because of you."

"What's that supposed to mean?" I stand up and head for my bedroom door. Maybe she'll take the hint and leave too.

"It means you blew it." She follows me to the kitchen, watching as I open the fridge. "And now he's hurt."

I remove a can of lemonade, ignoring the fact that Stacie is helping herself, acting like she lives here. Whatever.

"And you probably said something like, 'Nice girls don't do that.' Right?"

I nod as I pop the can open and take a swig.

"So how do you think that made him feel?"

"I don't know, but I'll bet you're going to tell me."

"He probably feels guilty for asking you now. He probably thinks you don't really like him and—"

"I do really like him," I say.

"Just not enough to—"

"I don't want to talk about this anymore." I set down the lemonade and make a run to the bathroom, trying to hide the fact that I'm crying, which is really weird.

"Elise?" Stacie calls through the door. "Come out, let's talk about this. I can hear you crying."

"Just go home," I tell her. "I'm fine. Really . . . just PMS. And I have to do homework. So I'll talk to you tomorrow, okay?"

"Okay, but you've got me worried."

"Really." I try to brighten my voice. "I'm fine." With the bathroom door locked, I sit on the edge of the bathtub, waiting for her to leave. After several minutes, she finally seems to take the hint and I hear the front door close with a thud.

Okay, maybe I really am having PMS. Or maybe I'm just really frustrated. Who knows? But honestly, Stacie is the last person I want to talk to right now. She just confuses me and makes me feel worse.

I emerge from the bathroom, go to my room, and open my

computer, but like I expected, there's no email from Asher. And I don't want to be the first one to write again. In fact, I'm starting to wonder if I've just been a total fool for letting myself fall for a guy who will probably never give up on his girlfriend. I'm halfway tempted to write him an angry email and tell him that we're finished. But that seems pretty lame considering that we never really got started. I mean it's not like we've been together. Not really.

I shut down my computer and climb into bed. Maybe I can simply sleep this broken heart off.

"Elise?" my mom calls.

I get up to see that it's almost seven. "I'm here," I tell her.

"Oh, I saw your car down there, but it was so quiet . . ." She studies me. "Are you okay?"

"Just a little bummed."

"More boy trouble?"

I kind of shrug. As I help her fix dinner, I tell her a bit more about Asher (not about the photos!) and about how I'm afraid he's just leading me on. "He'll probably never break up with Brianna."

"That's a possibility. And it might be that he's enjoying having the attention of two girls. Some guys are like that."

It's hard for me to believe Asher is really like that, but then again . . . I don't know. "Well, maybe I'll just go to the homecoming dance with Phillip," I say suddenly. "That would teach Asher a lesson."

"And Phillip seems like such a nice boy. Why don't you?"

"I think I will."

When we're done with dinner, I pick up the kitchen phone. Right then and there, with Mom giving me a thumbs-up, I call Phillip and tell him that I'd like to go to the dance with him. "I mean if you still want to."

"Sure," he says. "It'll be fun."

"Yeah, I think it will be." Okay, I don't tell him that part of the fun will be seeing Asher's face when I walk in with Phillip. But at least he'll get the message that I'm not going to be strung along like that.

As I get ready for bed, I think about calling Stacie—just to tell her that I'm sorry I fell apart and that I'm okay and that I'll see her in the morning. She did seem pretty worried about me, which is actually kind of sweet. But I noticed her sister is visiting tonight, so I'm sure Stacie's already forgotten about me. I can just explain things to her in the morning.

9

"But what about Asher?" Stacie demands as I'm driving us to school. She's still digging through my bag in search of gum, although I told her I don't have any. And she's mad at me because I just told her I'm going to the homecoming dance with Phillip, not Asher. Seriously, this girl needs to get her own life!

"What about him?" I say to her with disinterest.

"He's so in love with you, Elise. Remember the roses? The emails? You can't just give up on him like this." She tosses my bag down in disgust.

"I'm not giving up completely," I point out. "I'm just taking a little break."

"But what if Asher changes his mind? What if he's broken up with Brianna? What if he asks you to the homecoming dance now?"

I laugh. "Like that's going to happen."

"It might."

"Hey, it's sweet that you're so wrapped up in my crazy life, but don't worry, Stacie, it'll all work out. Phillip is actually a really nice guy. I was talking to my mom about him last night, and she thinks he's great. I do too."

Stacie lets a foul word fly.

"Hey," I say. "No cussing in my car."

"Sorry." She folds her arms across her front and slumps down.

"What's with you?" I ask. "You can't be that mad at me for agreeing to go to the dance with Phillip."

She doesn't answer. Fine. I need to focus on my driving anyway. Let her pout by herself—pity party of one. If she's so nuts about Asher, maybe she should go after him herself. Not that she's likely to get anywhere. In fact, I have a feeling he was never going to break up with Brianna in the first place. Mom's probably right—some guys just like thinking all the girls are in love with them.

I'm heading for Spanish when I feel someone grab my arm—tightly. I turn to see Asher with a hard-to-read expression. "We need to talk," he says urgently.

"Right now?" I glance around, worried that someone may be looking.

He firmly nods as he escorts me away from the classroom and toward a somewhat secluded corner near the restrooms. "What do you think you're doing?" he demands.

"What?" I peer curiously at him.

"I thought you were a *nice* girl."

"I *am* a nice girl," I shoot back. "What are you talking about?"

"That photo!" he hisses.

"I thought you liked the photo."

He kind of smiles, but suddenly scowls. "You never should've sent it to me. That was wrong! So wrong!"

"But you wanted—"

"Seriously, Elise. It was a stupid, stupid move. Brianna saw it, and now it's—"

"What's going on here?" Bristol asks as she emerges from the restroom. "A clandestine meeting of sorts?"

"No way." Asher growls at her.

"Definitely not!" I step away from him.

Bristol gives me a snooty look. "You're a real piece of work, Elise Storton—a real class act."

"Thanks," I snipe back at her. "Same to you."

"At least I'm mature enough to know that sexting is not only wrong, it's a punishable crime in this state."

"*What?*" I stare at her. "*Sexting?* What are you talking about?"

She laughs. "Oh, sure, play innocent. That'll work." The bell rings and she struts off.

"She's right," Asher says in a stern tone. "It *is* a crime."

"What are you talking—"

He holds up his hands and shakes his head, like he's finished with this conversation, and even more than that, like he's finished with me. Then he just turns and storms off.

Feeling totally confused and slightly freaked, I follow about ten feet behind him, wondering what on earth is going on. I know something is not right, but I have no idea what—or how. As I slip into my seat, I realize that being tardy is probably the least of my worries today.

It's hard to focus on Spanish verbs as I try to remember what the actual definition of sexting really is. They talked about it at my old high school last year, and I thought it meant sending nude photos or sexually explicit messages. I'm fully aware that I sent that stupid swimsuit photo of myself—which in hindsight was totally moronic—and I may have written things about how much I liked him or even said that he was hot. But *sexting*? I don't think so.

Class is almost over when a man in a suit comes into the room to speak to Ms. Sorenson. To my total horror, she points directly at me, then motions for me to come up to her desk.

"If you'll get your things and come with me, Miss Storton," the man says in a polite but firm tone.

I look at Ms. Sorenson, who nods. "Do as he says, Elise."

Once we're outside of the classroom, I start to freak. For all I know, he's some pervert trying to kidnap me. "I'm not going one step with you until I know exactly who—"

"I'm Detective Lewiston." He flashes a badge at me. "You are Elise Storton, right?"

"Right." I feel a deep-seated fear in the pit of my stomach.

"I want to ask you some questions," he tells me.

"About what?"

"Please, come with me."

"What's going on?" I demand. "What's wrong?"

"I'm going to place you under arrest for distribution of child pornography, penal code 33—"

"What?" I feel my knees get weak as he spews out some numbers and words, then proceeds to rattle off my Miranda rights as he takes my bag from me without even asking.

"Now, you can make this easy or difficult," he says as he escorts me toward the front of the school. "I wanted to be discreet, but I have handcuffs if we need them."

"No thanks."

We stop at the administration center, and he takes me directly into a counselor's office, just like this has all been preplanned.

"I'm Mrs. Rollins," a middle-aged woman tells me. "You must be Elise Storton."

I nod, but tears are filling my eyes and my legs feel like wet noodles.

"Please sit down." She motions to the chairs adjacent to her desk. "I'm the guidance counselor at Garfield High, and I've taken the liberty to call your mother. And I requested that Detective Lewiston stop by here before taking you down to the precinct . . . so we can talk."

"The precinct?" I ask.

"You are under arrest," the detective reminds me.

"But why?"

"For distributing child pornography," he repeats slowly, like maybe I'm not too bright. "Just like I told you."

"Otherwise known as sexting," Mrs. Rollins says in a weary voice. "You see, even when you send photos of yourself, it's still illegal if you're a minor or sending them to a minor. I thought all you kids knew this by now."

"But I didn't *do* that," I insist.

"We know for a fact that you sent a pornographic image of yourself to Asher Gordon," Mrs. Rollins says. "And according to Asher, someone else, not him, then forwarded that photo on to other students."

I feel sick to my stomach. How could he? Why would he? I want to die—just shrivel up and die.

"How old are you, Miss Storton?" Detective Lewiston asks me, although I can tell he already knows.

"Sixteen."

"That means you are still a minor. And that means sending that photo will be considered distribution of child pornography."

"But I had my swimsuit on," I say.

"Must've been an invisible swimsuit," he says as he writes something down in a notebook. "Maybe like *The Emperor's New Clothes*. My kids used to like that fairy tale."

"What are you talking about?" I ask him as Mrs. Rollins hands me a tissue. "It was a swimsuit, a real swimsuit."

"Sexting is a serious crime," he says. "And unless your counselor has anything else to say, I'm taking you downtown, young lady."

I look at Mrs. Rollins. "How can he do this? I haven't done anything. I'm innocent."

"That's right," the detective says. "Innocent until proven guilty. Want to come willingly, or should I get out the handcuffs now?"

"What if he's not a real cop?" I quickly ask Mrs. Rollins. "What if I'm being kidnapped and—"

"My partner's in the car," he tells us. "A female. But Mrs. Rollins is welcome to accompany us outside if you'd like." He nods at me. "That's actually a smart move, Miss Storton. Too bad you weren't smarter about distributing child porn."

It feels like the whole school is watching . . . and laughing . . . as Mrs. Rollins walks out with the detective and me. Then he introduces me to his partner, a woman named Officer Jones, who's in uniform. The car, although unmarked, does seem official in a drab-gray way. I'm about to get into the backseat, perfectly willingly because I want to get out of sight of my classmates, when Officer Jones tells me to put my hands behind my back.

"It's policy," she tells me as she handcuffs me.

I hear hoots and laughter from behind me, but I don't look back. I simply bend down and allow Officer Jones to help me into the backseat, where she proceeds to buckle me in like I'm a four-year-old. Then I lean my head forward and just cry. What is going on? Why am I being treated like this?

At the precinct, I hold up a card with my name on it and am photographed from all angles. Then I'm fingerprinted. Although everyone is polite, I am basically being treated like a criminal. So much for innocent until proven guilty.

Finally I'm placed in a room by myself to wait. What I'm waiting for is a mystery to me. Maybe they plan to blindfold and execute me. I'm not even sure I would care.

I tell myself that this is all just a bad dream, and anytime soon, I should be waking up. But then Detective Lewiston and Officer Jones come in.

"We'd like to get a statement from you," the detective tells me.

"Unless you'd rather wait to have an attorney present," Officer Jones interjects.

"My statement is that I'm not guilty," I tell them.

"So you didn't send that photo of yourself?" Detective Lewiston says. "Even though Asher says it's from you? You deny this?"

"I sent a photo of myself in a swimsuit," I say for what feels like the hundredth time. "I realize now that was a very stupid thing to do, but it's not illegal, is it?"

"A swimsuit photo that's really a swimsuit photo is not illegal, Elise," Officer Jones gently tells me. "But a nude photo, even if it's to your boyfriend—if either of you are minors—*is* illegal. Do you fully understand this?"

"Yes," I tell her, nodding. "I get that. But I didn't *do* that."

"Then tell us who did," she urges.

"No one," I say. "Because it never happened."

"In other words, you refuse to cooperate with us," the detective snaps at me. "In that case, I have better things to do." He stands and marches out. Officer Jones stays behind. Now she smiles, and suddenly I imagine good cop–bad cop scenarios.

"Listen, Elise, this will go much easier for you if you cooperate. We know that sexting seems acceptable to some teens. They don't fully understand the implications of the law. But first-time offenders can get off pretty lightly. Some community service, a class . . . no big deal. We might even be able to get your record expunged."

"But I swear I didn't send a nude photo of myself." I'm starting to cry again. "Why won't anyone believe me?"

"Then tell me who sent it, Elise." Her voice is growing impatient now. So much for the good cop.

"I don't know." I lean my head onto the table as new tears come. "This is all like a bad dream. Nothing makes sense."

"Who took that photo of you?"

"No one."

"You took it of yourself then?"

"No, there is no such photo."

"I can only help you if you're willing to help yourself, Elise. That doesn't seem to be the case." She stands.

I look up at her with blurry eyes. "I don't know how to help myself. All I want is to tell the truth."

She smiles. "That's what we want too. Just the truth."

"But I didn't do anything wrong. I mean I didn't do anything illegal. I know I didn't. I swear I didn't."

"Then you'll have to prove that, Elise. Because the evidence says otherwise. And you'll have to prove it in a court of law. If you won't tell me what really happened, I can't help you."

She stands there looking at me now, like she's waiting for me to pour out some big confession, but when I don't, she just shakes her head and leaves, and I am left alone in this stuffy room again.

After what seems like hours, my mom comes in. She is obviously very distraught.

"Mom," I say hopefully, getting up to go to her. But the way she looks at me—the anger and rejection in her eyes—stops me in midstep. It feels like I've just been slugged in the gut. I sink back down to the chair.

"I cannot believe you did something like this," she seethes. "I've never been so ashamed and humiliated in my entire life. That my daughter would lower herself to such a level, sending a nude photo—"

"But I—"

"Do *not* speak to me." She shakes her finger at me. "I was tempted to let you stay here in jail after they showed me that nasty photo." She shakes her head in disgust. "That a daughter of mine would—"

"*What* photo?" I demand. "What did it look like?"

"I think you know what photo, Elise. Now get up. Let's go."

"But I never—"

"Don't talk to me," she snaps. "Let's just go. I have a lot to do, thanks to you. I have to make excuses at work. I need to find an attorney, which won't be cheap. And the police want to escort us back to the apartment in order to confiscate our computers and cameras—" She gives me another withering look. "This is just way too much, Elise. I am so furious. I don't even have words to—"

"But Mom, I didn't—"

"*Shut up!*"

So I do. I just shut my mouth and am determined to keep it shut *forever*. Even if I'm being convicted of something I never did, or if I'm accused of sending a lewd photo, well, fine, just lock me up and throw away the key. I really don't care.

Detective Lewiston and Officer Jones follow us to the Tropicana Suites, and then they come up the stairs and instruct my mom to unlock our apartment. "You come and show us where things are located," the detective tells her.

"Elise will wait right here," Officer Jones says crisply. I stand by the front door, while the police, aided by my mom, proceed to confiscate our computers, Mom's camera, and even her cell phone, which I can tell is really ticking her off. Although she's not saying anything, she is seething mad.

"That should be it for now," the detective tells Mom. "And

you know the rules for posting bail. You signed the agreement. So don't be taking any unexpected family vacations or anything."

"Don't worry about that," Mom says in an irate voice.

As soon as the police leave, I go straight for my room. I wish I had a lock on the door, but since I don't, I simply slam it loudly. Naturally this infuriates my mom. And this time she doesn't hold back at all.

"You have to be the most ungrateful spoiled brat on the planet!" she yells. "When I think of how I pinched and saved to buy you that car, how I scrimped so you can have ridiculous things like your own cell phone, and this is the thanks I get—sending nude photos of yourself to—"

"I did *not* send—"

"I *saw* the photo, Elise!" she screams. "I saw the evidence for myself. It was sent *by you*! The photo was *of you*! You sent it to that stupid Asher Gordon boy you've been so crazy about! And I do *not* want to talk about it anymore right now!" She puts her hand to her forehead with a grimace, and I suspect she's about to have a migraine, which is not that surprising. I think I feel one coming too. I just stand there mutely and watch her storm out of my room, and this time *she* slams the door.

I've always considered myself a fairly upbeat person. And my faith in God has been a fairly stabilizing force as well. But suddenly it feels like I've been cast out into a very rough sea, with no lifeboat, no flotation device, and a bunch of sharks moving in to devour me.

Seriously, everything around me looks bleak and hopeless. Everyone at school thinks I'm a slut or a joke or worse. Asher totally hates me—I could see the disgust in his eyes. Stacie won't even talk to me. Phillip is probably embarrassed to admit he knows me, and I can count on the fact that we won't be going to homecoming together now. Even my own mother has turned her back on me—is humiliated by me. I didn't even do this thing that I'm being blamed for. But no one will listen to me.

Even when I make an attempt to pray, begging God to get me out of this mess, I get the feeling that he's not very sympathetic . . . like maybe he thinks I'm partially to blame for all this. And maybe I am . . . maybe this is what I get for trying to steal Asher from Brianna. And yet I know I'm innocent. *I never sent that photo!*

This must be how Hester Prynne felt in *The Scarlet Letter*. I remember reading that book in English Lit last year and thinking that it was so wrong and unfair. Hester's life was ruined and she was scandalized—she bore all the blame and shame—just because she was a woman and was slightly careless. Meanwhile the man, guilty as sin, simply went his merry way. I remember thinking then that if I were Hester Prynne, I would either run away or just kill myself.

Now, for the first time in my life, I seriously consider both of these options. There must be some way out—some escape from this mess previously known as my life. I consider how hard I've tried to make this move work. How I didn't give

Mom too much grief about switching schools, when any normal teen would've thrown a fit. And even though my dad is a jerk, I try not to be too bitter at him, and I've actually forgiven him for most things. I think about how I've tried to make friends—even spending time with a fourteen-year-old with an inferiority complex. Or how I try to be a Christian—how I pray about things and go to church.

But really, what is the point? For the first time, I wonder whether life is even worth the trouble. I honestly do not see how things will get any better. In fact, it seems highly likely they will get worse. How can I go on?

10

Dark and depressing thoughts chase me like hungry wolves through the night. I wish I could sleep and escape this torture, but it's like my mind keeps racing over details—replaying all that was said and done, trying to make sense of it. Like maybe I can solve this thing, but really I'm just going around in circles like a dog chasing its tail, or a hamster on an exercise wheel. Going nowhere fast.

Unable to sleep, I sit on the edge of my bed and feel so weary and beat up that I am utterly hopeless. Maybe it's the way a soldier might feel after being in battle. Shell shock, I think they call it.

Nothing about this day makes sense. And the more I try to wrap my head around it, the more slippery and confusing it seems. It's crazy—how can I be in this much trouble for sending a swimsuit photo?

Then I wonder—did Asher use Photoshop to alter my picture? Did he somehow remove my swimsuit and doctor the image to make it look like I'm actually naked? I'm sure it's possible to do something like that, but why would he want to? Furthermore, why would he forward something that skanky to everyone else? Wouldn't it make him look as bad as me? Wouldn't it get him into trouble with the law too? And if he did that, why would he act like he was mad at me? I remember the fury in his eyes. He was seriously outraged.

Nothing I can come up with makes any sense to me. And with no phone, no computer, and no one to talk to—just questions and confusion—it feels like my head is going to burst. I think I'll never get to sleep.

Finally it's three a.m. and I'm desperate for sleep. I tiptoe into the bathroom and open the medicine cabinet. I quietly search until I find an amber bottle of Ambien tucked behind a tube of HeadOn. I vaguely remember that the sleeping pills were prescribed for Mom a few years back. She'd been going through a rough spell at her old job. The date is expired, but I don't feel concerned as I pry off the lid and pour the small blue pills into the palm of my hand. There appear to be about twenty or so. More than enough to ensure a good night's sleep—or perhaps a permanent escape.

I fill the smudgy bathroom glass with water, sit on the toilet seat lid, and look at the blue pills in my hand. Really, what difference would it make if I were gone by morning? Who would really miss me? I close my eyes and let out a big sigh. Wouldn't it be easy? Just sleep my troubles away. End of story.

I take a deep breath, bracing myself to gulp down the pills and wash them down with lukewarm tap water. I think I can do this.

Suddenly it occurs to me that I haven't really prayed about today's trauma. Not specifically anyway . . . and not with faith. I wonder if it's even possible for God to unravel this mess. Or if he'd even want to. Right now, it feels like no one wants to help me. I am on my own . . . and everyone else is just waiting for me to go down.

The police want me to confess to what I didn't do. My mom wants me to shut up and disappear. Most of the kids at school want to ridicule me. Brianna and her friends probably want to kill me. Even the school counselor looked like she was tired of me—or stupid girls like me.

But I've known about God long enough to realize that he never gives up on us. I've read in the Bible that his love is endless and his mercy is new every morning.

I open my eyes and my hand, staring at the moist wad of pills in my palm. The blue dye is starting to stain my skin. I just stare at it in wonder. Instead of my hand, I see the hand Phillip drew in Art—the man's hand with the dark hole in the center. Jesus's pierced hand.

"Please help me," I pray quietly. "I need you more than ever right now. I know I'm innocent and you know I'm innocent. You know how it feels to be punished for something you didn't do. Please help me through this mess."

Feeling a flicker of strength, I stand up and lift the toilet lid. I dump the blue clump of pills inside the bowl and flush it, saying, "Amen." The blue stain remains in the center of my palm—but it's just a stain, not a hole.

As I return to my room, I feel a tiny glimmer of hope. Still, I'm as limp as a dishrag that's been squeezed and wrung out. I crawl into bed and close my eyes. I want to trust God for this. But more than that, I just want to sleep—to escape all this for a few hours. More than ever, I wish I could wake up only to discover it really was a dream this time—a very bad dream.

But when I wake up, it's to the sound of my mom's voice. Only it's not enraged like last night. Now her tone is flat and emotionless as she tells me to get up and get ready for school.

"*School?*" I repeat like she's nuts. "I am so not going to school."

"Oh yes you are," she tells me. "We're going right now so I can drop you off. You can pick up your car and bring it back home, and then you can ride the bus. And just so you know, I'm going to sell your car and—"

"*You're going to sell my car?*"

She looks at me like I've lost my mind. "You didn't actually think you were going to get to keep it, did you?"

I don't answer.

"I just hope it'll cover the attorney's fees." She scowls at me. "Now get ready. I do not want to be late for work."

"I'll help you pick up the car," I agree. "And you can do what you want with it, but I am *not* going to school. No way. No how. You can take me back to jail if you want. But I refuse to go back to that school—*ever!*"

She glares at me, and I'm pretty sure we're about to have our most serious argument ever, but I mean it. I am dead serious. I am not going back to school. Juvenile detention or prison or hard labor—anything would be better than the humiliation that's waiting for me at Garfield High.

"Fine then. It's your life and you seem intent on ruining it. Go ahead. You probably *will* end up in jail, Elise. And this time I won't bail you out."

The drive to school is silent—the kind of silence where you feel like you really could cut the air with a knife. But at least we're there early enough to avoid being seen. The parking lot's been unlocked, but only a couple of cars are there, including mine. Mom drives straight toward Bonnie Blue, but when I see my car, I feel sick inside. There's a long scrape on the driver's side—it starts at the front fender and goes clear to the end of the car.

"What did you do to your car?" Mom demands as we both get out and stare at the damage.

I run my hand along the scar, feeling the deep indentation of the gash, and a new lump develops in my throat. "Someone obviously keyed it," I say in a hoarse voice.

Mom actually swears now. This is something I've heard her do only a couple of times, and always in relation to my dad.

"Get it out of here," she growls at me. "I have to go to work." She slams the door to her car and drives off fast. I get into my car, and for a moment I consider driving off fast too. I think maybe I'll not only drive fast, but I'll go someplace far away. I could shoot down to Mexico or up to Canada or maybe just straight off a cliff.

Instead I drive to my grandma's house. Thinking she's already heard my story by now, since Mom usually tells her everything, I brace myself for her disappointment as well. But I know her wrath—if any—will be short-lived. Or at least this is what I tell myself as I knock on her door. I can hear Millie barking, and I hold my breath, waiting for the door to open.

To my relief, Grandma smiles and hugs me. "What a nice surprise, Elise. What, no school today?"

Millie seems happy to see me too, jumping and acting like I'm going to take her for a walk. Something about this little scene just gets to me, and I break down and start to sob. With her arm wrapped around me, Grandma guides me into the house and seats me at her kitchen table. Without even asking, she mixes me up a tall glass of chocolate milk and sets it in front of me. How do grandmas know to do things like this?

I take careful sips and slowly calm myself until finally I'm able to talk. But the story spills out of me in one long sentence, and by the time I'm done, Grandma looks almost as confused as I feel.

"You sent this boy a photo of you in your swimsuit?" she repeats—for clarity, I'm sure.

"Yes. I know that was stupid. But he sent me a photo of him without a shirt on and asked for a similar photo."

"But you did have the top of your swimsuit on?"

"Of course!"

She slowly nods as if she's trying to take this in. "But you were arrested for sending naked photos of yourself?"

"A naked photo. Just one . . . as far as I know. But it was forwarded around school so everyone saw it." I take a final gulp of chocolate milk. "But I never sent it. And I never had one taken. Never in my life!"

"Oh yes you did, dear."

I blink. "What?"

"When you were a baby. I took a couple of shots. You were perfectly beautiful." She smiles. "You still are."

I stand up and go rinse my glass, setting it in the dishwasher since I know she likes that. "Thanks."

"So back to this little dilemma, Elise. Where did the photo come from?"

I take Millie onto my lap as I explain my theory about Photoshop, and Grandma nods like that makes sense.

"Yes, I've heard of that happening," she tells me. "But can't that be proven by an expert?"

I feel a smidgen of hope. "I would think so."

"Did the photo look like it had been tampered with?"

"I never actually saw the photo."

She frowns. "You never saw it?"

I just shake my head.

117

"Well, that's just not right. I would think if someone arrested you for something, they should show you the evidence."

"Maybe they were waiting until I was in court."

"No, that's not right." She goes for her phone. "Let me call Wally. He's a retired lawyer friend of mine, and he's always willing to give me free advice." She winks at me like she's sharing a secret. As she calls Wally, I notice she's dressed differently. She has on old jeans and an old white shirt, which I suspect might've been my grandpa's, and her hair is tied up in a scarf. Upon looking more closely, I notice she has splotches of bright blue paint here and there.

"I'd appreciate it if you called me back when you get home, Wally. My granddaughter is here with a complicated legal problem and we could use some advice. Thank you very much." She hangs up and turns to me with a smile. "I'm sure he'll get back to us as soon as he gets in, Elise."

"What are you doing?" I ask her. "I mean it looks like you've got paint on you."

She gives a sheepish grin. "Can you believe it? I'm painting my bedroom."

I look at her with wide eyes. "No way. I thought you were never going to change a single thing about this house. I thought you said it was perfect."

She chuckles. "Oh, I suppose it is perfect. At least that's what your grandpa always thought. Maybe early on in our marriage I agreed. But I think a part of me always wanted to make a change." Her forehead creases. "Although now I'm not so sure." She motions to me. "Let me put Millie out back and then you can come and tell me what you think."

In the master bedroom, I try not to look overly startled when I see the wall color. It's an intense turquoise blue—like something you might find in a set of kids' felt pens or Stacie's nail polish kit. "Wow, that's really bright, Grandma."

She nods. "It's a bit much, isn't it?"

"Maybe." I look around the bedroom, which like the rest of the house is fairly neutral, but nice. "I've always loved this house just the way it is," I tell her. "You know, it's really retro. Sixties decor is hot."

"Do you know who decorated this house, Elise?"

I sort of shrug. "I just assumed you and Grandpa did."

"Do you remember that this was Grandpa's house before he married me?"

"Yeah, I guess I kind of remember that."

"His first wife, Lois, was an interior decorator. She did this entire house. That's why it's so well done and professional looking."

"Oh."

"And I suppose a tiny part of me resented that all these years. Oh, I liked it too. But I think I've always wanted to make my mark on it. And now that Grandpa is gone, well, I decided to just go for it. Now I'm not so sure."

"So why turquoise?" I ask.

She heads for her closet and pulls out what looks like a comforter set. It's kind of a tropical-looking print with shades of turquoise and lime green. "I fell in love with this," she tells me. "It reminds me of when Grandpa and I went to Hawaii for our thirtieth anniversary."

"It's pretty."

"I thought I'd like a turquoise blue room, sort of like *Blue Hawaii*, but now I think it's a little overpowering."

"Maybe so." I point to a soft aqua shade that's also in the fabric of the comforter set. "What if you went with something more like this?"

She studies the color. "You know, I think you're right." She frowns at the buckets of turquoise paint. "I guess that was a waste of money."

I look at the turquoise and remember what I do when I paint with acrylics. "Why can't you just get some white paint and lighten it up?"

"Brilliant!" She nods eagerly.

"And I can help you." Suddenly I'm hoping to distract myself from the anxiety that's gnawing away at my stomach. Maybe I can lose myself in a project and pretend that nothing is really wrong.

"What about school?"

"I'm not going back there." I firmly shake my head. "I told Mom I'd rather do prison time than return to school. She said she doesn't care." I feel tears coming again. "She's so mad at me, Grandma. I've never seen her this mad—not ever."

"Well, she'll cool off. In the meantime, you can help me get the right color and then we'll just paint our troubles away."

Grandma decides to send me to the paint store while she finishes masking off the trim and preparing the room. I explain the color challenge to the paint guy, then together we figure out how much white paint it'll take to make the color right. Finally we end up with a very soft shade of aqua, which I think Grandma will like.

When I get back, Grandma offers to start lunch for us. "You go and put some of the new color on the wall," she tells me. "We'll see if it works."

As I paint a large square of pale aqua, I block out everything else, and for the first time since my arrest, I feel like I can almost breathe normally. The color reminds me of a calm tropical sea, and I imagine myself swimming in it . . . on and on until I'm far, far away from my troubles.

"That's perfect," Grandma says as she comes into the room. "Absolutely, perfectly perfect."

"I like it too," I tell her. "And if it's okay, I'd like to keep painting. It's really relaxing."

She laughs. "Maybe it's paint therapy. At least for you anyway. The truth is I wasn't enjoying it much myself."

She gives me some old clothes to wear, hands me the scarf from her own head, and returns to fixing us lunch. I continue to paint . . . and to block out all else. When I take a lunch break, I make her promise not to peek at her bedroom until it's done.

"I feel a little guilty," she admits as I'm heading back. "Like I'm taking unfair advantage of a bad situation."

"I like your paint therapy theory better." It really is therapeutic, and as I paint, I decide that maybe I'll just drop out of school and go to work as a house painter. I'll bet they make good money too.

But by the time I finish the room around six o'clock, I'm not so sure. All my muscles ache, and I'm in serious need of a long, hot shower. The results are totally worth it, though. "Don't come in yet," I holler out the door.

"Don't worry, I'm starting to fix dinner now. Wally is coming over to join us."

I start cleaning up, packing up the paint things, removing drop cloths and masking tape, and scrubbing my hands. I put her furniture back where it goes and even put the comforter set on her bed before I clear all the painting things out. Then I call Grandma to come and see.

"Oh, Elise!" she exclaims. "It's beautiful. It's much better than I hoped it would be." She hugs me. "Thank you, thank you, thank you!"

I can't believe how happy this makes me. I can almost totally block out what's really going on in my life. Or maybe I'm just going into denial.

She points to her bathroom. "Now you get yourself cleaned up. Wally will be here soon. I made lasagna, his favorite."

As I'm showering in her oversized bathroom, I look at the walls and wonder if that blah beige might actually be better in pale aqua too. Maybe I can make an arrangement to stay with Grandma indefinitely—just paint her whole house one room at a time.

"We have the right to see the state's evidence against you," Wally tells us as we're finishing dinner.

"We?" I question. "Meaning you'll represent me?"

"If you want me."

I nod eagerly. "Of course. I'd love to have you as my lawyer."

"I'll let Elise's mother know what's up," Grandma tells him. "In fact, she should be getting home from work about now. Why don't I give her a jingle to let her know that you're here and you're okay?"

I want to remind her that Mom probably doesn't even care, but instead I tell her to call the landline. "Remember, our cell phones were confiscated by the police."

Wally makes a note of this. "We'll get to the bottom of this, Elise."

"So you believe me?" I ask incredulously.

"Of course I believe you. You're my client." He grins as he shakes my hand.

"I'm telling the truth."

He nods. "I know you are. And I have a good sense about these things."

I hear Grandma in the kitchen. She's informing Mom that I'll be staying with her for a while, and it sounds like my mom doesn't put up a fight. Grandma tells her about Wally too. Finally she lowers her voice, probably thinking I can't hear. "She's your daughter, Denise. It's your responsibility to believe in her. We all make mistakes—you know that as well as anyone—but you're making an even bigger mistake to believe Elise would do something like that. She's obviously been framed. With or without your help, we plan to get to the bottom of it." She says a pleasant goodbye and hangs up.

Wally smiles at me. "You know, I'm an old guy, but I've got a pretty good idea about some of the things mean girls can do to other girls. It's usually related to jealousy or some kind of love triangle. I strongly suspect there's another girl at the bottom of this little scandal."

I tell him a little bit more about Brianna and how Asher had been trying to keep our relationship undercover.

"She found out, didn't she?"

I just nod.

"I think there are lessons all the way around in cases like this. And I'm sure by the time we're done, you'll be all that much wiser for it, Elise."

"I hope so."

"You should see what a painter she is," Grandma tells Wally as I begin to clear the table. She chuckles. "If you didn't think I was too forward, I'd invite you to see what she did to my bedroom." She calls out to me in the kitchen. "Come on, Elise, let's show him your handiwork."

Wally is impressed with both the color and my painting skills. "I might want to hire you to repaint my living room."

"I was thinking maybe I should paint Grandma's bathroom to match the bedroom."

"Ooh!" Grandma claps her hands. "I'd love that!"

When I finally get to bed tonight, wearing one of Grandma's nightgowns, I am thoroughly tired. So utterly exhausted that I don't even think about my arrest or criminal record or upcoming trial. I just say a prayer, close my eyes, and fall asleep.

11

On Wednesday afternoon, I take a break from painting Grandma's bathroom when Wally arrives. His plan is to chronologically record everything I can remember that happened leading up to my arrest. He also takes down phone numbers, Asher's email address, and anything else he can think of that could relate to this case.

"A good lawyer is part detective," he tells me. "Or else you can think of it as putting a puzzle together. It takes a lot of pieces to get the full picture."

I'm not so sure that the picture is getting any clearer to me, but I do my best to cooperate with his questions. He tells me he's filed for copies of evidence and my arrest documents and statements.

"Well, that's about it for now," he says as he gathers his things up. "But if you think of anything else—no matter how small—that seems in any way connected to your case, write it down and get it to me."

I promise to do that, then return to painting the bathroom while he and Grandma head for the backyard with iced tea. It's around four when I finish painting, and not wanting to disturb them to wash out the brushes and rollers, I go around to the front yard instead. I'm just finishing up when I hear someone calling my name. To my surprise, it's my old friend Hilary—the very person who first introduced me to Asher, although that seems like a lifetime ago now.

"Hey, Elise," she says as she comes over with her mom's poodle. "What are you doing here?"

"Just visiting," I say casually. "Doing some painting for my grandma."

"How's school?"

I study her expression, trying to decide if this is a suspicious inquiry or just curiosity. Finally I decide to just be honest. "It's not so good," I tell her as I set the roller in the clean pan. "I guess I'm kind of taking a break."

"Really? They let you do that?"

"Under the circumstances, I don't think they mind too much."

"What circumstances?"

I quickly tell her how someone tried to frame me by sexting a guy. "A guy you happen to know," I say like it's no big deal. "Asher Gordon."

Her eyes grow wide. "Seriously?"

I just nod.

"So who did it? Do you have any idea?"

"I have a lawyer and we're trying to figure it out. He thinks there's a jealous woman involved, which makes me think it's Asher's girlfriend Brianna. But we're still gathering evidence. The police take sexting very seriously," I explain. "I was arrested and everything."

"I remember when something sort of like that happened in middle school. You didn't go to Webster, did you?"

"No, I went to Kennedy."

"Well, there was this big scandal at Webster when I was in eighth grade. Not for sexting exactly, although that was kind of involved, but for cyber bullying."

"What happened?"

"This girl Summer really hated this girl Rachel, so she and her friends went onto MySpace and some other sites and started saying really mean stuff about Rachel. They made up all these skanky stories, and everyone at school was reading them and believing them and forwarding them. They'd email Rachel and text her stuff, and they set her up to write back. Then they'd circulate it around the school. It was horrible."

"Did they get in trouble?"

"Yeah, but not until Rachel hung herself."

"She *hung* herself?"

Hilary nods. "I guess she just couldn't take it anymore."

"I kind of know how that feels," I admit.

"But you wouldn't hang yourself, would you?" Hilary looks alarmed.

"To be honest, I did have thoughts of suicide."

Her hand flies to her mouth.

"But I think I'm past that now. Mostly I want to get to the bottom of things."

Her dog is whining and tugging at his leash now, ready to continue the walk. "Well, good luck, Elise. I hope you figure out who did it."

"Me too." I give the last brush a good shake, then gather the tools and go back into the house. I sort of remember hearing about a girl who killed herself a few years back. But I didn't remember the part about cyber bullying. It makes me wonder—what is wrong with some kids? Why would they take something so hurtful and push it so far?

Suddenly I wish I had my laptop so I could do some research into all this stuff. Just how widespread is it? And what is being done about it?

I find Grandma and Wally in the kitchen and tell them about what Hilary just told me and how I'd like to do some investigation. "Except that the cops still have my laptop."

"You can use my old computer if you like," Grandma offers. "It's a bit of a dinosaur, but once it warms up it's not so bad."

"And do you mind if I use the phone to call a couple of friends?" I ask. "I'd like to ask some questions, see if anyone can figure this thing out."

"Great idea," Wally tells me. "Make sure you take good notes. Get times and dates when you can. And ask anyone you speak to if they'd be willing to give a deposition if needed."

I go into the den, which used to be Grandpa's favorite hangout, and turn on the old PC. While it's warming up, I call Stacie's cell phone. But instead of hearing her voice, I'm sent straight to voicemail. "Hey, Stacie," I begin, "this is Elise and I'd like to talk to you. But I'm staying at my grandma's for a few days." I give her the number and ask her to call back as soon as she can. "It's really important," I add.

Next I call Phillip, and he actually answers. "Elise?" he says with what sounds like hesitation, like he doesn't really want to talk to me.

"Hi, Phillip," I begin carefully. "I'm sure you know what happened by now."

"I know you got arrested for sexting Asher Gordon." His voice is edged in anger.

"That's how it appears," I tell him. "But that's not really the truth."

"What is the truth?" Again he sounds irked, and like he's in a hurry.

"I'm happy to tell you the truth," I say, "if you're willing to hear it. You sound like maybe you're busy."

He lets out a sigh. "No, I'm not busy. But I'll be honest with you, Elise. I was pretty shocked when I, uh, when I saw that photo."

"That photo!" I explode. "Yes, I keep hearing about *that*

photo. But I've yet to actually see it. Even when I was arrested, no one, not even the police, showed it to me. And—"

"You're saying you haven't seen it?" He sounds skeptical now.

"Of course I haven't seen it. There is no such photo. Not for real anyway. I suspect that someone used Photoshop to change a photo of me—" I consider my words. It's not that I want to lie, but maybe I don't want to lay all my cards on the table just yet. "Like a swimsuit photo that's been airbrushed to make the image appear naked."

"Elise, *the image*, as you call it, didn't appear to be naked—the image *was* naked."

"How do you know that for a fact?" I ask. "I mean you've never actually seen me naked, have you?"

He doesn't answer.

"I mean for real," I shoot at him. "I don't mean an image that's not really me."

"Okay." He sighs. "Let's say that image isn't you. Or that it's a photo that's been Photoshopped. In fact, you made me curious. Maybe I'll just take another look. I know enough about Photoshop to know if something's been messed with."

I cringe to think of him looking at that photo.

"And you say you haven't actually seen this photo?"

"Right. The police took my computer and cell phone as evidence—"

"Don't you know anyone who has a computer? Or you could go to the library."

"As a matter of fact, I just turned on my grandmother's computer. But how can I find the photo on that?"

"Well, it's been removed from some sites, but it's still around."

"What do you mean it's still around?"

"I mean it will continue to circulate, Elise—good grief, it might circulate until the end of time. Don't tell me you don't know that something like this could make it hard to get into college or get a job."

I groan. "Thanks for all the encouragement."

"I'm just being honest."

"So, seriously, how do I go about pulling up this photo?" I ask. "Or maybe you could send me—"

"Are you nuts? Do you not get that sending a photo like that is a crime? You're a juvenile. I'm a juvenile. Do you think I want to get—"

"Right, yes, I'm sorry. I wasn't thinking."

"Apparently that's been going around."

"Look, Phillip, I'm sorry. I can tell you've been hurt. And just in case you were wondering, I have no intention of making you take me to the homecoming dance."

He laughs. "Yeah, right. I wasn't too worried."

"Just so you know, this hasn't been a walk in the park for me either. Do you have any idea how painful this is? I actually considered suicide the first night that it—"

"No way!" He actually sounds concerned.

"I'm sorry, I shouldn't have admitted that. But it's true.

I've been devastated by this. It's like no one will believe me. Thankfully I've got a good attorney and my grandma is standing by me. But for a while . . . well, it just seemed so hopeless."

"Okay, I found a MySpace page that's still got the photo on it." He quickly gives me the address, which I write down then navigate to. Suddenly there is this image—a girl with long dark hair like mine, flowing over one bare shoulder. Her head is bent down and sideways so I can't see her face, just her chin, but her body is in full view. And even though I don't stand in the mirror and study my naked physique, I have to admit that her curves look familiar. Yet I know—*that is not me.*

"Did you find it yet?" he asks.

"I found it," I say quietly. "But it's not me."

"Who is it then?"

"I have no idea."

"Why was it originally sent from your phone?"

"My phone?" I try to grasp this. "I thought someone sent the photo online, through email."

"Oh, trust me, it's been online, through email, on MySpace and a bunch of other places. You're getting around, Elise."

"It's *not* me!" I yell. "I swear, with God as my witness, it's *not* me."

"Okay," he says quickly. "Calm down."

"*Calm down?* Would you be calm if someone did this to you?"

"Did what? Sent me a naked photo? Actually, I did receive

a naked photo, Elise. Just like half the kids in school. And I wasn't too happy about it."

"That's not what I mean, Phillip. Imagine if someone faked a naked photo of *you* and sent it to everyone with *your* name on it. And you knew it wasn't you and that a photo like that had never been taken, but no one believed you. How would you feel?"

"I don't know."

"Well, trust me, you wouldn't like it."

"Okay, let's say I believe you, Elise. You never had a photo like that taken. But I'm looking at it now and I can honestly say I don't see any signs of Photoshop on it. Either this person was really a pro or someone's lying."

"Of course someone's lying," I tell him as I stare at the horrid photo with my name plastered beneath it. "That is *not* me." Yet even as I say this, it's like my mind is starting to play tricks on me and I think maybe it is me. Maybe someone took a photo and I didn't know it. Like when I was getting out of the shower. But why would I look so posed? And dry? "I feel like I'm losing my mind," I tell him. "Or like I'm going to be sick to my stomach. Or both." I turn off the screen. "I can't stand to look at it." Now I'm crying. "What am I going to do?"

"Don't cry," he tells me in a soothing voice.

"But I feel so trapped. How can I prove this isn't me? I wish there was some kind of DNA or fingerprinting they could do with a photo like this."

"The police got all your stuff, right?"

"Yes. My cell phone and laptop and my mom's camera . . . anything they felt was evidence."

"So if that photo was sent from your phone—"

"Which seems impossible."

"Well, that's the charge, right? That's what everyone at school was saying—that you sent it to Asher's phone. You need to remember who had access to your phone. Maybe the police will find fingerprints."

"This is making my head hurt," I say.

"Sorry, but you wanted someone to believe you, Elise. I was just trying to piece things together."

"Yeah, I appreciate it. Actually, just seeing the photo— which is totally disgusting—is kind of helpful. I mean I know it's not me. And there must be a way to prove it."

"Take another photo."

"Oh, great idea, Phillip. Then I could send it to everyone and say, hey, look, this is really me."

"Sorry. Bad joke."

"Extremely bad."

"Well, life hasn't been easy for me either. Some people, including the police, assumed that I was your boyfriend, and I've been questioned about whether I knew you were sexting Asher or whether you ever sexted me."

"I'm sorry. That's awful. But it's not like I could do anything to prevent this."

"So tell me, Elise. If you didn't do this, and I want to believe you didn't . . . The truth is I was pretty shocked. It really didn't seem like you at all. But if you didn't do this, who did?"

I remember the swimsuit photo and realize the only fair thing to do is give full disclosure. I tell Phillip that I'd been crushing on Asher and how we'd been exchanging secret emails. "Remember, you warned me to be careful."

"Yeah . . ."

"Well, Asher had asked me to send photos. So I sent a regular one. Then he sent me one of him—like a swimsuit photo, you know?"

"Uh-huh?"

"In exchange, he asked me to send a swimsuit photo."

"And you did?"

"I'm ashamed to admit I did. I wasn't going to, but Stacie kept egging me on, saying it was no big deal and how everyone does that."

"Stacie-who-is-barely-out-of-middle-school Stacie?"

"Yeah. But really, it seemed pretty harmless."

"Right . . ." I hear the skepticism returning to his voice.

"Look, I'm just trying to be honest with you."

"Well, you've really fallen into a tangled web, haven't you?"

"It sounds like you think it's my fault."

"I didn't say that, Elise."

"You didn't have to." I turn the computer screen back on, cringing when that image reappears. "I'm sorry to have dragged you into this," I tell him as I blink back tears.

"That's not what I meant."

"I know, I know," I say quickly. "Guilt by association and all that stuff. I don't blame you if you never speak to me again. I'm sorry to have bothered you," I choke out then hang up.

I just stare at that naked girl as hot tears streak down my cheeks. Will this ever end? Will it ever go away? Or is Phillip right—will an image like this dog my heels for the rest of my life?

12

"Would it be okay if I drove over to the apartments to get some more clothes?" I ask Grandma after I turn off the computer. I'm sick of hearing sad stories, sick of taking peeks at that photo, sick of my life in general.

"Yes, I was wondering about that too. But maybe I should take you in my car. Your mom said she doesn't want you driving the Mustang."

"Right . . ." I nod and try not to seem too hurt.

"I've told her that she can't sell that car until we've gotten to the bottom of this," Grandma says as she reaches for her purse. "I said that would be like judging someone guilty without a fair trial."

"She already did that," I point out.

"Yes, well, she's under some stress."

"What else is new?" I say glumly as we go outside.

"Why don't you drive, dear?" Grandma hands me the keys.

As I back out of the driveway, I try not to look at my car. But I see that horrible deep scratch and cringe. Poor Bonnie Blue.

Before long, I'm cruising down the highway, and although it's a small thing, I realize it feels good to drive again. At least I can still do something right. When I get to the apartment complex, Grandma wakes up from her nap and offers to wait in the car for me.

"I'll hurry," I promise.

She waves her hand. "Just put the windows down a bit and take your time."

As I'm going up the stairs, I meet Stacie on her way down, taking out the trash. "Stacie!" I cry happily. "I'm so glad to see you."

"Uh, yeah," she says quickly. "I gotta go dump this."

"Sure. I'll go with you," I say as I trail behind her to the dumpster. "So what's up? How's it going? Did you get my message?"

She tosses the bag in and turns to me with a frown. "I'm not supposed to talk to you."

"Who says?"

"My mom."

"Your mom?" I cock my head to one side. This is pretty weird since, other than nagging Stacie to help with chores, the woman is pretty laid-back.

"Yes. My mom heard about what you did and—"

"How did your mom hear about it?"

Stacie shrugs. "I don't know. Stuff gets around."

"But—"

"Look, I don't want to get in trouble, okay? And if I'm seen talking to you, I could be in big trouble. I know about the police coming here and everything. And don't forget I took that swimsuit photo, so I'm sure they'll think that I might've . . . well, you know, taken that other one."

"The police took my mom's camera," I point out. "That will show them you didn't."

She nods, then glances over her shoulder like she expects the cops to come crashing down on us at any moment. "I gotta go."

"Fine." I shake my head. "I thought you were my friend."

She doesn't respond to this but simply hurries up the stairs and back into their apartment. Still, something about this doesn't feel right. I don't get why her mom would suddenly get involved. I happen to know that her mom's done a few things that aren't exactly legal. Not that I'm going there. And usually she seems to turn a blind eye to Stacie and what she's doing. Even my mom has mentioned this, saying that for a fourteen-year-old, Stacie has way too much freedom.

I let myself into our apartment. I'm halfway surprised that Mom didn't change the locks. I quickly gather a few things, shoving them into a bag, and then I leave, locking the door behind me. This place never really felt like much of a home anyway. But even less now. I wonder if I'll ever be welcomed back.

In fact, as I hurry back to Grandma, I wonder why I don't just ask to live with her and transfer back to my old school. Oh, I'm sure my "past" might follow me there, but at least I might have some friends (like Hilary) who may believe in me. However, I can't forget that Hilary is dating Asher's cousin. Who knows what kind of a spin Asher could be putting on this story?

That makes me think I need to put him on my list of people to question. Brianna too. And Bristol and Lindsey and all the rest of them. Somehow I need to get the truth out of someone. Because I have no doubt . . . someone knows. Maybe a few someones.

As I drive Grandma home, I tell her about my odd conversation with Stacie. "I'm thinking maybe the only way to get to the bottom of this might be to return to the scene of the crime."

"To school?" she asks with interest.

"Just to investigate. In fact, I was thinking maybe I could go back to my old school . . . maybe even live with you . . . if Mom doesn't want me back."

She chuckles and pats my knee. "Oh, your mom is going to want you back, Elise. She probably does already. But she's stubborn and it hurts to think you'd do that. But once she figures things out, I have no doubt that she'll want you back."

"But what if she doesn't?" I ask with uncertainty.

Grandma laughs loudly now. "Then I'll be happy to keep you. And you can go to school wherever you please."

I let out a sigh of relief.

"However, I do like your plan to return to the scene of the crime. Wally is doing what he can, but he can't get inside there and sniff around like you can, Elise."

"And if I tell myself I'm returning to go undercover . . . not to go back to school there for good . . . well, maybe I can get through it."

"Don't expect it to be easy," Grandma warns. "You'll have to have thick skin."

"I know."

"You know what Grandpa used to tell your mother?"

"What?"

"What doesn't kill you only makes you stronger."

I just nod. But the truth is . . . I'm not totally sure this couldn't kill me. I think about that poor Rachel girl who hung herself in middle school. Then I remember my own dark night and that wad of blue sleeping pills. But I also remember the stain in my palm and how it reminded me of Jesus's nail-pierced hands. And I think maybe with God's help . . . maybe I can do this.

Of course, that's not what I'm thinking as I drive myself to school the next day. Grandma got permission from Mom for me to use the car to get to school. But Mom made it clear that was all I was to use it for. Whatever. I think I need the extra long drive this morning anyway. To pray and to just get a grip.

I take the note that Grandma wrote me (excusing my absences) to the administration office. It figures that Bristol works there first period.

"You're back?" she questions. Then, giving me a haughty look, she takes Grandma's note that's carefully written on good stationery, holds it between her thumb and forefinger as if it's contaminated, and walks away. I watch to make sure she puts it in the basket where it should go before heading to class. While her reaction to me isn't surprising, it's a little unnerving and one more indicator of what I can look forward to for the rest of the day.

As I slip into my seat in English Comp, I feel eyes on me and hear snickers. My plan is to ignore them as I remind myself that not only am I innocent, I am on a mission. I'm a reconnaissance spy who's willing to endure hurt and humiliation toward a specific goal—to unravel this little mystery.

My plan is to confront Asher and Brianna—and not privately either. I intend to find them in the midst of their friends at their favorite table in the cafeteria. There, with God and the whole world watching, I will question them. My strategy is to catch the diabolical pair totally off guard—an ambush of sorts, and possibly my best chance to get to the truth. Or so I hope . . . and pray.

In the meantime, I will keep a low profile. I will act the way everyone expects me to . . . like a cowering, whipped puppy, eyes cast downward, basically a wimp. Then, when the timing is right, I'll hold my head high as I look Asher and

Brianna straight in the eye and demand to know the truth. It could work.

Avoiding eye contact, I make my way into Spanish. Like a frightened mouse, I slip into my seat, open my book, and just stare blankly at the pages in front of me. It's been a long, hard morning and I'm already questioning my plan—as well as my own strength. I've discovered it's not easy to be a reconnaissance spy. It's like I'm playing the role of whipped puppy-girl and actually starting to feel like it. Like I really should tuck my tail between my legs and go whimpering back to Grandma's house.

Then I remind myself of the Bible verse (in my own version), "As a girl thinks of herself, so she becomes." So instead of thinking poor, sad, beaten-down loser girl, I imagine myself as Joan of Arc. Yes, they might burn me at the stake, but at least I will go down with my head held high—nobly—and with God at my side.

When the bell rings, I remain at my seat, pretending to finish up my grammar assignment, but really waiting to exit by myself once the room is emptied. When I get up to leave, I see that Ms. Sorenson is watching me with curious eyes.

"How are you doing, Elise?" she asks in an unexpectedly kind voice.

I try not to look too shocked. "Okay, considering everything."

She nods. "Yes, I heard about what happened. I must admit I was surprised. You don't seem like that—"

"I didn't send that skanky photo," I say with conviction. "It's not even me in the picture. Someone did it to get me. But I plan to find out who's responsible and then inform the police."

She blinks. "Really?"

I nod. "It won't be easy, but that's my plan."

She smiles now. "Well, good luck with it."

I let out a sigh. "Yeah, I'll need it." With my head held high, I head for the cafeteria. But the closer I get to it, the more it feels like I'm Joan of Arc heading to my own execution.

You can do this, I tell myself. *You are strong. You are innocent. God is on your side. You CAN do this!*

It's high noon and time for the showdown. I march over to where Asher and Brianna are holding court at their elite table, and with my hands on my hips, I stare at them. "I want to know who sent that photo," I say loudly.

They look at me with their phony blank expressions and slight air of boredom, their typical response to most things. Like they're too cool to care about anything besides their little clique of stuck-up snobs.

"Get over yourself," Lindsey says with exasperation. "Because we are." This is followed by snickers and giggles.

"I know that one of you is responsible," I continue. "I just want to know who did it . . . and why."

"We all know *you* sent the skanky photo," Brianna tells me with narrowed eyes. "Everyone in this whole school knows it came from *your* phone, which only shows how totally stupid you are. And that's why you were arrested, loser girl."

"I did *not* send it," I say loudly. "Someone stole my phone and sent the photograph to frame me, and I want to know who is responsible."

"Someone *stole* your phone?" Bristol repeats dramatically. "You seriously expect us to believe that someone stole your phone?"

"Yeah," Brianna continues. "And perhaps that same someone carried your phone off to a secret location and snapped a photo of a naked girl with it—a naked girl who happens to look strangely like you—and then that someone sent the photo to Asher's phone. And then that same someone slipped the previously stolen phone back into your purse without you noticing." She shakes her head. "Not only are you stupid, loser girl, you're insane."

I point to Asher now. "You know who sent that photo to you, don't you? Not only that, but you know why."

He just shakes his head, but in a way that says he thinks I'm a pathetic nuisance and he wishes I'd just disappear.

"And you forwarded it too," I continue. "Right?"

"I did not," he states. "That's a lie."

"Then who forwarded it?" I demand. "It's your phone, Asher, you should know. Who forwarded it to the whole school?"

He just shrugs.

I point to Brianna. "You forwarded it, didn't you?"

She just shrugs too. Like monkey see, monkey do.

"Well, that was a crime too," I tell them. "Because whoever forwarded that is criminally responsible for dispersing child pornography—guilty on even more counts than I've been charged for because you sent it to so many phones and websites. And I plan to make sure the police investigate both of you equally to find out which of you is responsible."

"Maybe Asher's phone was stolen too," Brianna says in a taunting voice. "Maybe that same *mysterious someone* who stole your phone got ahold of Asher's phone. Maybe there's a mysterious phone thief at our school—the little phone bandito with the black mask, lurking down some dark hallway. Why don't you go try to find out where the phone bandito is?"

Everyone laughs as if this is terribly funny.

"Leave us alone," Brianna tells me coldly. "Don't you get that we don't want to be seen with a slut like you? You're embarrassing, loser girl."

"And if you think that photo of you was hot, you're totally delusional," Bristol adds. "Your body is as lame as you are, loser girl."

"Get lost, loser," Lindsey adds.

"This isn't over," I tell them. "The truth will come to light."

"The truth is you're pathetic," Brianna says in that same bored tone that she started out with. "And boring." She turns away and they all laugh.

Okay, I tell myself as I turn and walk away, maybe I did lose round one. But I am not giving up. I am so not giving in. I will see this thing through to completion. But I have no appetite for lunch now.

I feel the heat in my cheeks and my stomach is tied into a knot, so I go for a walk and pray, feeling like God is my only friend. And I ask myself, why is that not enough?

13

"You're not wanted here," Bristol tells me when I try to take my seat at my old table in Art class.

"This is where I'm sitting," I announce as I set my bag down on the table with a plop. "Thanks anyway."

She gives me a look that I'm sure is meant to wither me to nothing, but I'm not going there. I look straight back at her. "You know, you'd be really pretty if you didn't go around with that look on your face all the time."

I hear Phillip chuckling as he comes up behind me.

"And you'd be really smart if you knew how to keep your clothes on," she tosses back at me. "Especially with a body like that."

"Hey, I thought her body was hot," says a guy across the room. "I wanted to ask her to pose for us when we start doing figure drawing."

Mr. Hanson clears his throat from the work table at the

front of the room where he's helping someone cut a mat. "Please turn your attention to your projects, class."

As I work on the pen and ink, I try to strategize my next move. But I'm afraid I don't really have one. Well, except to encourage the police to track down the jerk who forwarded the naked photo to everyone. I'll ask Wally to follow that up for me.

Class is just about over when I sense someone watching me. I look up to see Phillip staring.

"What's wrong?" I ask him.

"Just thinking about something."

I kind of shrug then return to my picture.

"Elise?" he says quietly.

I look up again. "What?" I ask with a little irritation.

"You have a pretty good tan, don't you?"

I frown at him. "What are you talking about?"

He reaches over now and pushes up the sleeve of my shirt to my upper arm. "See how tan you are?"

"Please don't tell me you're going to lecture me about skin cancer, because I have about all the stress I can take in my life right now."

"No, this isn't about skin cancer. I'm just pointing out that you appear to have a really good tan."

"So?"

"So, how long have you had it?"

"How long?" I stare at him like he's losing his mind. I notice that both Katie and Bristol are looking on with curiosity. "I don't know," I say. "I mean I spent a lot of time by the pool this summer. I guess I've had it for several months. But it's starting to fade some. What's your point?"

He leans down and peers straight into my face. "My point is the photo of the naked girl didn't look tan. She looked kind of pale—"

"It sounds like you really studied that photo," Bristol teases him. "And here I thought you were such a principled guy, a Christian too, right?"

"Christians have eyes, Bristol." He smirks at her. "We are human, you know."

"Oh, I'll bet you are," she taunts him in a flirtatious way. "Really, really human."

"So, Phillip," I persist, "what *is* your point?"

"My point is that girl in the sleazy photo didn't have a tan. She didn't have tan lines either. She was really pale."

Katie kind of nods now. "He's right."

"You saw that photo too?" I ask her.

She makes an uncomfortable smile then nods.

"Do you get what I'm saying, Elise?" Phillip presses.

"Yes," I say eagerly. "And you're absolutely right—and totally brilliant!"

"Wait a minute," Bristol jumps in. "Just because you don't have tan lines in the photo doesn't mean it's not of you."

"Then how do you explain my tan?"

"Maybe you've been to a tanning booth."

"No way!" I shake my head. "That's freaky."

"Or maybe you use self-tanning lotion."

"That stuff stinks."

She narrows her eyes at me. "Or maybe you took that photo last winter when you were white as a ghost."

"That's easy enough to prove," Phillip tells me. "It was your camera that took the photo, right?"

I frown. "So they say."

"Well, it's not hard to prove that. The date the photo was taken will be recorded. The police probably know exactly when the photo was taken by now. If it was recently, you can prove your innocence by your tan." He chuckles. "Innocent by way of melanoma."

"That's a sweet thought." I roll my eyes at him, but at the same time I seriously want to hug this guy. Yet I don't want to overwhelm him when we're just barely friends again. "I really can prove I'm innocent now. This is fantastic. Maybe you should consider detective work as a career option."

"You can only prove your innocence if the photo's recent. I'll bet that it's not," Bristol says. "I'm guessing it's something you did for some other unsuspecting guy you were crushing on last year. Someone from your old school. Asher told us he's got his cousin checking up on you, finding out just what kind of girl you really were before you moved here and started acting like Little Miss Goody-Goody."

"I'm not a goody-goody," I protest.

She nods. "I must agree with you on that account, Elise. So you might as well give up your little innocent act. Because no one's falling for it."

Phillip gives me a slightly empathetic look as the bell rings. I thank him again for making his observation. He smiles. "You know, Elise, I'm actually starting to believe that photo really wasn't you."

"Hopefully I can convince everyone of the truth," I say as we leave the art room.

Bristol laughs. "And if you pull that off, I recommend you take up drama, Elise, because we're always on the lookout for talented actresses."

I'm totally antsy to get out of here now. I want to call Grandma and probably Wally too. Maybe even my mom if she's willing to speak to me. But my next two classes seem to last for eternity. Even so, I can't afford to skip them. I've already gotten behind by missing a few days. And with all my other problems, I'm pretty sure I don't want to add failing grades or truancy to the list.

Eventually the final bell rings. I blast out of school, rush to my car, and try not to speed as I drive back to Renaldo. If only I had my phone, I would gladly pull over and just call everyone. As it is, I feel like I'm living in the seventies . . . or whenever it was PCP (pre–cell phone).

Unfortunately, Grandma's not home when I get there. Millie happily barks and greets me, which means Grandma probably went somewhere besides the store or post office, since she usually takes Millie on these trips. Suddenly I realize I'm starving, so I consume a hefty chunk of leftover lasagna and an apple. Then I just frantically pace back and forth in the kitchen, wishing my grandma would hurry.

Finally, I can't stand it. I go into the den and turn on the old computer, waiting for it to warm up so I can pull up the MySpace page where that horrible photo is still posted. I study it closely and realize Phillip was absolutely right. The girl is ghost white with absolutely no tan lines. Even if strange lighting was used, I would never look that pale. Not since last winter anyway.

Just to prove this to myself, I close the door to the den, remove my shirt and bra, and look down at myself, then compare what I see to the photo. I had never really thought the photo was me—except for the brief fear that someone caught me getting in or out of the shower—but it's such an enormous relief to see the difference in skin tone. I notice that there are some other minor discrepancies as well.

"What are you doing?" Grandma demands when she walks into her den to find me topless.

"I can explain," I tell her as I grab my shirt and hold it over myself.

"Elise?" Her eyes are wide, and she stares at the computer screen and then at me. "What on earth are you doing?" Her tone is alarmed, and I can only imagine what's going through her head.

"Grandma," I say calmly, "I'm just trying to prove my innocence."

"You have a very strange way of doing that," she says.

"Look." I peel a part of my shirt away to reveal my tan lines from the top part of where my suit would cover me. "I have a tan." Then I point to the computer. "That person does not."

She blinks and looks more closely at the photo. "You know, I believe you're right."

"This could be my proof," I tell her.

"What should we do?" she asks. "Take a naked photo of you?"

I consider this. "That might be considered child porn too."

She nods. "Let me call Wally and get his opinion."

While she does this, I get dressed.

"Wally is going to call the police. He thinks that, if you're willing, he will recommend that a female officer along with a dermatologist expert examine you and perhaps even take photos—but not pornographic ones, of course. He thinks with that evidence as well as the dermatologist's expert opinion, it might be useful in court." She smiles now. "If it goes to court. Wally is feeling hopeful that your charges will be dropped."

"That's the best news I've heard in days," I tell her. "Well, beside Phillip pointing out my tan in Art class."

"Who is Phillip?"

I tell her a little bit about him. "He's actually a really great guy. We'd gone to church together and we were even going to go to the homecoming dance together . . . before all this happened."

"You can't still go to homecoming?" she asks sadly. "When is it anyway?"

"Tomorrow night," I tell her.

"Too bad. This Phillip sounds like a very nice boy."

About an hour later, Wally calls back and wants to talk to me. "The police are willing to take your suntan situation into consideration," he tells me. "I'm trying to get an appointment set up for Monday at the precinct."

"That long?"

"Is your tan fading fast?" he asks with concern.

"I don't know. Maybe I should go sit by the pool this weekend and beef it up a little."

"No, don't do that, Elise. They might think you were working on it just to prove yourself innocent."

"Okay." I bite my lip. Every day that this thing drags on feels like a year to me. I so want it to be over and done. But I know I need to be patient.

"Anything else I need to know?" he asks. "How did your undercover investigation go?"

"Not as well as I'd hoped. Although it does seem obvious that either Asher or Brianna was responsible for forwarding that photo. They didn't admit it, but I could tell by their expressions that they knew. My guess is that Brianna did it when she grabbed Asher's phone from him. But wouldn't the proof show up on their phones?"

"Yes, and this is a point I already made to the DA. But I'll follow it up. Asher's phone and maybe Brianna's should be seized for evidence too."

"That seems fair."

"Well, you hang in there, kiddo. I promise you, we will get to the bottom of this."

"Thanks. I appreciate it."

After I hang up, Grandma asks me if I've told Mom about my new evidence.

"Well, I haven't really had the chance," I admit. "But I'd like to. Do you think she'd listen?"

Grandma smiles. "Yes, I'm pretty sure she's ready to listen. I had lunch with her today and she's cooled off."

"Cooled off, but still thinks I'm guilty?"

"Let's just say she's worried about you, Elise. She knows how much you liked that boy. And she knows about the other photo you sent him. It's not a huge stretch to think you might've gone all the way with your photos." Grandma sighs. "Remember, darling, your mom wasn't exactly a saint at your age."

I nod as I realize this is true.

"So it's easy for her to jump to conclusions about you. But I told her you're a good girl—a good girl who's attracted the attention of some not so good girls . . . or boys."

"And she listened?"

"She tried."

"So what do I do now?"

Grandma hugs me. "As much as I hate to let you go, I think it's time for you to go home. Your poor mother is miserable without you. Do you realize how important you are to her?"

I frown. "It sure didn't feel like it when she practically threw me out."

"Well . . . think about how you felt when the boy you

thought you were in love with—that Asher Gordon—let you down. Now, we don't know for sure that he's really guilty of everything that's happened, but it's possible. Think about how quickly your feelings went from true love to . . . well . . ."

"Hatred?"

"Sometimes it's the ones we love the most who can hurt us the worst—whether it's intentional or accidental or even innocent. And when we're deeply hurt, we tend to lash out."

I nod. "Does everyone get wise when they get older?"

She grins. "The smart ones do."

I pack up my things, put them into my car, thank Grandma for her shelter in the storm, and head back to the Tropicana Suites and my mom.

As I'm carrying my second load of stuff up the stairs, I spot Stacie peeking out her front window. I dump my stuff in my room and go knock on her door, but she doesn't answer. I knock again. Louder this time. But still she doesn't answer. I know she's there and I can even hear her.

"Stacie," I yell. "Come out and talk. I'm moving back home. I've got some good news about this case. I just want to tell you—"

"Keep it down," she says as she jerks the door open. "My mom's taking a nap."

"Oh, sorry. I just wanted to tell you my good news."

"What news?" She looks suspicious.

"I can prove that photo wasn't of me," I say.

"How?"

I laugh. "Well, Phillip is the one who pointed it out, but the girl in the photo is pale as a ghost, and I have a pretty good tan as well as tan lines. Also, when I looked more closely, I noticed a few other differences. I'm thinking the human body is kind of like a fingerprint. Every single one is different. And my attorney is setting things up to have an expert do an examination and comparison. It will probably prove my innocence."

"Oh." Her expression is hard to read.

"Aren't you happy for me?"

"Well, yeah, of course."

"Do you know how horrible this week has been?"

She kind of shrugs.

"It's like everything was taken from me—my reputation, my dignity. Sometimes it even felt like my sanity was on the line. And now maybe I'll get it back."

"Right . . ." Stacie glances behind her. "I should probably go."

"I just thought you might like to know."

Stacie smiles now, but it seems a little forced. "I'm glad for you, Elise. Really, I am."

"And I can give you a ride in the morning."

"That's okay. I already have one."

"Oh . . . okay."

"See ya!" she says as she closes the door.

"See ya." I just stand there a moment and wonder. Maybe

I'm wrong about getting my life back. What if everyone treats me like I'm still guilty—even after I prove my innocence? What if I've been smeared and the stain isn't going to go away? What if I have to live with suspicious glances and suggestive innuendos for the rest of my life?

14

"Grandma said I should come home," I tell Mom as she enters the apartment. "I hope that's okay."

She sort of shrugs as she sets her purse on the small table by the front door. "Yes, I told your grandmother that I've cooled down some." She frowns at me. "I'm still upset by this, Elise. Don't get me wrong."

"I can understand why you'd be upset," I say, trying to remember all that Grandma had told me earlier today. "But I do have good news."

Mom looks suspicious. "Good news?"

I can't help but grin as I spill out the whole story of tan lines and pale bodies. "My friend Phillip is the one who noticed I had a tan during Art today," I finally say. "He's got kind of an artistic eye, you know. He pointed out that the girl in the photo—the girl who is *not* me—is ghostly white. I mean, seriously, she could be into vampires, she's so pale."

Mom sits down on the couch with a thoughtful expression. "I barely looked at that photo," she admits. "It made me feel sick to my stomach . . . broke my heart . . ."

"I'm sorry, Mom," I say. "But I swear to you it wasn't me."

"I do remember that paleness, which actually made it seem even worse in a pornographic way—not that I'm into porn. But I remember seeing some photos when I was a teen and they kind of looked like that. Creepy. And I really couldn't understand how you . . ." She looks up at me with tears in her eyes. "How you, my sweet little girl, could do something like that." She shakes her head. "It was like someone pulled the earth out from under me. Can you understand that?"

I sit down next to her and put my arm around her shoulders. "I totally understand that, Mom. It's how I felt when I found out that someone had done that to me—that they'd gone to the trouble to take a photo, send it to Asher, and make it seem like it was really me."

"But who would do that, Elise?" Mom reaches for a box of tissues on the coffee table—an almost empty box, which tells me she's gone through a lot of them this week. "Who would take off her clothes and pose for a photo like that and then pretend to be you? Who is that wicked, that depraved, that immoral, that . . ."

"Skanky?"

"Yes. All that and more. Who do you know like that?"

"I honestly don't know who is in that photo, but I think I

162

know who sent it. I mean it seems like it must be Brianna, Asher's girlfriend. But I have no idea how she did it."

"Well, just proving that it's not you takes a load off, Elise."

"If you have any doubts, I'll strip naked and you can look at me."

Mom laughs then blows her nose. "Spare me."

I confess about how I actually took off my shirt to see for myself. "And Grandma walked in and saw me."

"Oh my goodness!" Mom laughs even harder now. "What did she do?"

"I thought she was going to have a heart attack. But I explained what was going on and she totally got it. I even showed her my tan lines—discreetly. And she could see the difference. Not that she ever doubted me."

Mom sighs. "I wish I had believed you too, Elise. I'm really sorry about that. Can you forgive me?"

I hug her. "Of course I can. Absolutely."

"So what's the next step in this mess?" she asks as we go into the kitchen to work on dinner.

"Wally—you know, my lawyer—is setting up an appointment with some experts. He's pretty sure he can get the case dismissed without going to court."

"And maybe we can get our phones and things back?" she asks.

"I hope so. It's hard being shut out of twenty-first-century technology."

She chuckles. "I know what you mean. I was thinking

that exact same thing today. I was tempted to buy one of those cheap phone card phones but told myself to just be patient."

As we're eating, Mom asks me to explain my theory on how all this happened. "I just need to understand it better," she tells me. "I've gone around and around in my mind trying to make sense of it."

I begin by telling her how Asher and I had our secret online relationship. "Remember I told you how he didn't want to break up with Brianna until after the homecoming dance—"

"When is that anyway?"

I sigh and fork my pasta. "Tomorrow."

"And I assume you're not going."

"That's right," I say glumly.

She shakes her head. "Okay, continue with your story."

I explain about how the emails got more romantic and how I was enticed to send the first photo. "But it was just me, fully clothed, smiling. No big deal."

"Where did you get the photo?"

"Stacie took it."

"And you emailed it to him?"

"Yes. And then the romance seemed to be heating up. He sent me a photo of him without a shirt on." I feel my cheeks growing warm. "He's pretty good looking, Mom. I mean seriously, he kind of resembles Matthew McConaughey. Except that he's a jerk."

"But you didn't know that then."

"No, of course not. I thought he was . . . you know . . . Prince Charming. And I respected that he wanted to keep his promise to Brianna by taking her to homecoming."

She nods. "Yes, I even fell for that."

"After he emailed me his slightly steamy photo, he urged me to send him a swimsuit photo. I wasn't going to do it."

"That would've been smart."

"But then I kind of let Stacie talk me into it. I mean she kept telling me it was no big deal and that everyone does it, and finally she just wore me down."

"Never listen to a fourteen-year-old."

"Yeah. So I sent that photo. And then it was weird, I didn't hear much back from him." I try to remember how this went down exactly. "But it's always been kind of up and down with us," I admit. "I remember this one time when I broke our secrecy rules and actually talked to him in a normal way, not acting like I was mad or anything. It was almost like he was glad to talk to me. He even walked me to lunch, and I got the feeling that things had changed, like he was actually going to announce to Brianna and everyone that we were secretly involved. But then he emailed that same day, begging me not to talk to him anymore. Not until after the dance."

Mom holds up her fork. "Now, doesn't that seem just a little bit fishy to you?"

"What?"

"What you said about him being surprised and happy to see you and walking with you. But then he emails something totally different?"

"I figured Brianna had thrown a fit. Probably threatened something. So he was just trying to keep her happy until the dance."

"But why? Why should a young man be that concerned about keeping his fishwife of a girlfriend happy when he's so in love with you?"

I sit there and ponder this . . . but I have no answer. "I don't know."

"Okay, tell me what happened next."

I have to think hard now. "I wish I had my computer so I could read the actual emails," I say. "But as I recall, what happened next was that he pressured me to send him a really sexy photo. He said it would help him to get through the next week—you know, because we couldn't be together. But I wouldn't do it."

"Wouldn't do what?" she asks.

"Send a skanky photo—no way was I going to do that. And I told him so."

"Did he continue to pressure you?"

"He sent one more email that same day, saying I wasn't who he thought I was. He seemed hurt. But come to think of it, he was like that a lot."

"Like what?"

"You know, kind of hurt, like I'd offended him. But I guess I assumed it was part of the game."

"The game?"

"I'd act mean to him in front of people at school."

"And why was that?" Mom looks totally bewildered.

"I was trying to do what he wanted by keeping my distance and acting like I hated him."

"You acted like you hated him?"

"That's what he wanted me to do, Mom. It was our cover-up."

"Oh, Elise, don't you get it?"

Okay, it's like this little light is starting to glimmer. "What?"

"He tells you by way of email to avoid him, ignore him, act like you hate him, right?"

"Right."

"But when you see him in person, he acts different—like he's glad to see you and he likes you and he has no problem being seen with you, or else he seems hurt when you're mean to him?"

"Yeah, it was like that. Kind of schizophrenic. But I thought it was because, like me, he was kind of confused. We were playing this game, but the rules kept changing."

"Because he wasn't making the rules."

"He wasn't?"

Mom's eyes are wide. "No. I'll bet it was his girlfriend emailing you, Elise."

"No . . . I don't really see—"

"Think about it. What does this girl want?"

"Besides Asher?"

"She wants to keep you away from him. She wants you to push him away, to act like you hate him, to refuse to speak to him—because if you do that, if you play the game according to her rules, she wins. Don't you get that?"

I slowly nod. "Actually, I do."

"Brianna was doing the emailing right from the start."

"And she's the one who wanted me to send photos?"

"Yes . . . and being a smart girl—a wicked smart girl—she started out with just a regular photo. She was just warming you up."

"But don't forget, Mom," I remind her. "I didn't send that nude photo. It wasn't me."

Mom frowns. "This is where it gets a little murky."

"Maybe Brianna was mad that I didn't fall for her nasty little plan," I say. "Maybe that was her final goal—to get a nude photo and totally humiliate me with it—so she went about it another way."

Mom nods. "That could be right. She might've found someone who looks a little like you, asked her—maybe paid her—to pose nude." Mom frowns now. "But how did she manage to get your phone to snap that photo?"

I think about this.

"Do you have any classes with her?"

"No."

"How about one of her friends?"

"Bristol!" I say suddenly. "I have Art with her. We sit at the same table. And my purse is always there, but I have to get up to get paper or supplies or to make a mat or whatever. My purse is there unattended a lot of the time."

"So perhaps Bristol snagged your phone."

"Yeah. And she might've gone to use the restroom. Maybe it was all prearranged that this person would be there, ready to pose." I make a face. "Is that gross or what?"

Mom nods.

"But it does seem possible. And Bristol keeps arguing with me about this in Art, saying how I'm so guilty and how I'll never get out of it. It's like she's too involved, you know?"

"Like she's trying to cover her trail?"

"Exactly."

"So . . ." Mom says slowly, "how are you going to get Bristol and Brianna to slip up and admit to all this?"

"I'm not sure. But I think the place to begin is with Asher."

"Why Asher?" Mom asks.

"I'm not sure, really. I guess I want to make certain he's really not involved. For one thing, there are the criminal charges. It would be unfair to implicate him if he's really been in the dark this whole time." I shake my head. "I mean it's kind of hard to believe that it really wasn't him. I never even questioned it. Even the email address sounded authentic. And the photo. It's just so weird."

"Well, it happens all the time, Elise. The internet is the perfect place for someone to assume someone else's identity. It makes sense that Brianna would have photos of her boyfriend. And anyone can set up an email account with any name on it."

"But I can't believe I was so gullible."

"Next time you won't be," Mom says as we start clearing the table.

"Hopefully there won't be a next time."

"Well, I'm just glad that we're getting this figured out, Elise. The sooner it's over and done with, the happier I'll be."

"Me too."

But as I load the dishwasher, I'm not so sure it'll ever be over with. Not completely anyway. I'm afraid that I'll never have my life back. Not like it was anyway. How do I replace all that's been stolen from me? I almost ask Mom this question, but she's been through so much already. There seems no point to burden her with it right now.

As I do my homework, I find myself wishing for a normal life again. I mean normal as in being something of a wallflower and being the friend of a slightly immature fourteen-year-old and going to church and hanging with Phillip. I would gladly welcome all of that again if I could turn back the clock and erase all the emails and photos. Only I'm getting worried that it's not even possible. It's like what's been done is done and nothing I can say or do—even proving my innocence in a court of law—will ever undo it.

Because of the research I did at Grandma's (as well as the lectures I received from the police and guidance counselor), I'm worried that electronic technology and the long arm of the internet could drag that nasty photo with my name on it clear into the next century. It seems possible that even my great-grandchildren would find out about what happened this week—and what would they think of that? That they had descended from a slut?

Perhaps I'm not so different from Hester Prynne—marked for a life of judgment and criticism. Whether it's getting into college, a new boyfriend, a job application, or whatever, I could be followed by this forever. I imagine a red *P* branded on my forehead—*P* for pornography.

15

When I get out of my car, which, like me, is marked—but hopefully not scarred for life—Phillip walks across the school parking lot toward me.

"How's it going?" he asks.

"Okay."

"What happened to your car?" he asks when he notices the mark.

"I think someone keyed it."

"Did you report it to the police?"

"I told my lawyer about it and it's included in the report."

"Because traces of paint can stay on a key for a long time."

"Really?" I look curiously at him. "Are you seriously considering a career in crime prevention or something?"

"I like cop shows."

I laugh as I sling the handle of my bag over my shoulder.

"I tried to call you, but I'm guessing your cell phone is still in jail."

I nod. "I'm just starting to get used to being without it."

"Anyway, I was thinking about the dance tonight . . ."

"The homecoming dance?" Okay, this is like duh obvious, but I can't think of any other response.

"Well, I asked you to go with me and you said you would . . . but then all that mess happened . . . and I was thinking it's not fair that we let whoever did this to you dictate our lives. Seriously, Elise, why should we let them spoil our fun? So, I know it's late notice and you'll probably say no, but will you go to the dance with me?" He smiles hopefully.

"Seriously?"

"Absolutely."

"Sure. Why not?" Then I question myself. "But isn't it a formal dance?"

"We don't have to go formal. I'm open to whatever."

I consider this. Do I want to show up at this dance as a misfit? Considering all the attention I've had this week, I don't think so. "Can I borrow your phone?"

"Sure." He pulls it out of his pocket and hands it over. I call my grandma and quickly explain the situation.

"Oh, Elise, that's wonderful. But what will you wear?"

"I have no idea."

"Well, I'm just full of ideas. How about you meet me at Macy's after school? I'll get there early and do some scouting around."

"It's a date." I hand the phone back to Phillip. "Okay, I guess it really is a date. And I expect to have a formal dress. Do you have something to wear?"

"Just this old tux of my dad's—kind of retro, you know. My mom had it altered to fit me. It looks okay."

"I'll bet it looks better than okay."

He grins. "This is going to be fun."

"I hope so." So I pray that it will be fun . . . and a normal evening. But as messed up as my life has been lately, I wonder what the chances are.

As soon as Spanish class ends, I head straight for Asher. "We need to talk," I tell him in a no-nonsense voice.

"What?" He looks suspiciously at me.

"I need to ask you some questions."

"Why?" His eyes narrow. "So you can tell the police more lies about me?"

"Lies?" I glare at him. "You should talk about lies."

"I so don't get you, Elise." He makes a fist then relaxes it. "You seemed so nice at first, but Brianna's right, you're a total b—"

"You seemed nice too, Asher. You wrote me a whole bunch of really nice emails and—"

"I've never emailed you in my life."

"Really?" I look curiously at him and almost believe he's telling the truth. But my plan is to get him to figure it out himself. "Then who was it who emailed me over and over in *your* name? Who pretended to be madly in love with me? Who insisted we have a secret romance so Brianna didn't find out about us? Who asked me to avoid you or to treat you like a sworn enemy whenever we were in public?"

"Huh?"

"Don't you remember the times I ignored you? Or said mean things to you? Or acted like I hated your guts?"

"I thought you did hate me."

"It was our cover-up."

"*Our* cover-up?" He looks really confused now.

"Yes. You asked me in email after email to keep our love secret from Brianna—you said you couldn't break up with her until *after* the homecoming dance. Remember?"

He blinks then shakes his head. "*What?*"

"You emailed about how much you missed me and begged me to send photos of myself. You even sent a photo of yourself. A beach shot—you were shirtless and showing off your muscles."

His frowns. "And did you? Did you send photos of yourself?"

"Just online. The first one was a normal shot—as in fully clothed. And then, only because you begged, I eventually sent you a swimsuit photo. But that's where I drew the line. I *never* sent a naked photo to you or anyone else. And I never will."

"Then who sent your photo to me?"

"It wasn't my photo. Don't you get it? It wasn't me."

"Who was it then?"

"Good question. But I can prove it wasn't me. My attorney is getting everything set up to do just that. And then my case will be dismissed. Unfortunately, it won't be so easy for you and Brianna, because you really did distribute child porn, Asher. When you forwarded that photo—supposedly of me—you became a real criminal. And when you—through your email—begged me to send naked photos of myself, you incriminated yourself even more. The police have all this evidence in my computer—"

"I know," he says quickly. "They already came to my house and took my computer and my cell phone."

I feel a wave of relief.

"But, honest, Elise, I didn't do that. I *never* emailed you. I swear. Not once. And I wasn't the one who forwarded the photo either."

"But it was on your phone."

"And it was sent from your phone."

"Then we've both been framed," I tell him. "Three guesses as to who was involved." I glance over to the restroom, the same one Bristol popped out of the other day. I hold up one finger. "Brianna is suspect number one. But it's possible she had accomplices." I hold up another finger. "Bristol is number two." I hold up all three fingers now. "And I'll bet Lindsey is number three." I shrug and put my hand down. "But I'm just guessing."

"But why? Why would Brianna do something like this?"

I can't help but laugh. "Why? Are you serious?"

"Yes. This whole thing is so extreme. So over the top."

"Not to mention middle school."

"Yeah. I don't get it. Why would Brianna do this? If she actually did it . . . and I still have a hard time believing that. But she's not stupid. She must've known she'd get caught. Why would she push things so far—and where would she get that nude photo?" I can tell by his face that he wants to believe Brianna's incapable of something like this. Who can blame him? "Tell me why she would do something like this."

"To hold on to you." I sigh. "So she decided to play this internet game—a game she thought she could win. Her goal was to keep you guys together until the homecoming dance. What she planned to do beyond that was—oh yeah, her plan didn't end there, did it? She also wanted to humiliate me so completely that I'd be too embarrassed to show my face here again. Well, she was wrong about that."

"But why did she target you?"

I hold up my hands like this is one of life's great mysteries. "I don't know. Somehow Brianna got the crazy idea that you were interested in me." Okay, as I say this, I realize how I'm leaving myself wide open because I bought into Brianna's little scam. Like a gullible sap, I responded to those emails. I admitted I loved him—or so I thought—and Brianna probably intended to use those emails to humiliate me.

"But how do you know for sure it was Brianna?" he challenges me. "How can you prove it?"

I shrug. "It's just that she's the most obvious suspect."

"Just like you were the most obvious suspect for sending that photo?" He scowls now, like he thinks I'm trying to scam him. Whatever.

"Anyway," I say quickly, "I just thought you should know. At least when the police start to question you, you'll have a little heads-up about the emails. Whereas I had no warning—I was totally blindsided." I turn to leave.

"Wait," he calls, following me.

"Why?" I ask in exasperation.

"Because Brianna was right about one thing."

"What?" I fold my arms and wait.

"Actually, two things."

"Yes?" I let my impatience show.

"I was into you."

"Oh . . . and the other thing?"

"I was going to break up with her."

I shrug. "Too bad you didn't, huh? You could've saved us all a whole lot of pain. And jail time." Now I walk away. Really, it's all I can do. Having him standing there, saying that, with that expression . . . well, it could almost undo me. Except that I remember too well how he spoke to me in front of his friends, believing the worst of me, condemning me, humiliating me. Really, I am so over him. Or at least that's what I'm telling myself. A small part of me pities him.

As I walk to the cafeteria, I decide that the ball is in his court now. What he'll do with it is anyone's guess. I can tell he's not convinced that Brianna is behind all this. Still, I think he might have a better chance of extracting the truth from her than I would. Although that girl is as slick as Teflon—nothing seems to stick to her. I'm pretty sure that Asher, to spare his own name and reputation, will have to bring her down.

Instead of getting some lunch, which I so could not eat right now, I head for the library, where I find a vacant table and sit down to write out all the things I said to Asher, as well as the things Mom and I put together last night. I know it's not real evidence, but perhaps it will help my case. Anyway, I will hand this all over to Grandma to give to Wally.

"What's up?" Phillip asks quietly as he sits down beside me at the table in the library. "I was looking everywhere for you."

"Why?"

He frowns. "I thought Brianna might've hired a hit person to take you out."

"Very funny." I kind of laugh.

"I'm not kidding."

"Oh . . ." I glance around to see if anyone is listening, then, in a hushed voice, I replay my confrontation with Asher.

"Wow." Phillip nods. "Impressive."

"We'll see. The big question is will he believe me? Or will he remain under Brianna's spell?"

He shrugs. "Hard to say."

"And hard to imagine that he'll stand up to Brianna. I'm afraid he might try to take the fall for her."

Phillip frowns. "You honestly think he'd take the fall for her—after the way she's tricked him and lied and everything?"

I chuckle. "Well, the guy who was writing me those emails—aka Brianna Cole—sounded like he might. He sounded so noble and heroic and devoted, unwilling to break his promise to his girlfriend."

"Except that he was having an online affair behind her back," Phillip reminds me.

"Good point. And if it makes you feel any better, I'm not too proud of myself for getting pulled into that scheme."

"But you're out now?"

I nod. But the look on Asher's face (when he told me the two things Brianna was right about) is stuck in my head. It seemed he was telling the truth. Still, I believe it's a case of too little too late.

"So are we still on for tonight?"

"Totally," I assure him.

"I wonder if Asher and Brianna will still go."

"That would be ironic, wouldn't it? I mean either way—whether they go or don't go."

"How's that?"

"Ironic if they *didn't* go after how much effort Brianna invested in keeping them together, and ironic if they *did* go after all the stunts she pulled on him."

Phillip nods. "I can't wait to find out how the story ends."

"Now I want to see if I can get any information out of Bristol in Art. I can't help but think her friends are in on this game. So no matter what happens between us, just stay cool, okay?"

"Sounds like fun."

Bristol is clearly ticked at me when she walks into Art. Her eyes are narrowed, locking onto me as she makes her way across the room, almost like she's stalking her prey. I vaguely wonder if she could be carrying a weapon.

Like Phillip and me, she's here a few minutes early—as if on a mission to hunt and destroy. "So there you are." She glares at me as she sets her bag on the table. "I don't blame you for hiding out, you little coward."

"I'm not a coward," I respond calmly.

"I know what you're trying to do to Brianna. Everyone does now."

"What's that?"

"You've been trying to break up their relationship. Right from the start too."

I roll my eyes. "So says Brianna."

"She showed me the emails *you* wrote to him. I saw for myself how much you wanted him. It made me sick . . . and then I just had to laugh. You are pathetic."

"How did Brianna get into Asher's email?" I ask as Katie comes in and takes her regular seat. As usual, she's early, but I can tell she's having second thoughts now. Phillip just tosses her an understanding smile.

"News flash, moron. They happen to be *going* together," Bristol says in a hostile tone. "They know each other's passwords."

"And how does Asher feel about Brianna sharing his personal email with her friends?" I ask.

Bristol laughs in a mean way. "Considering that Asher was cheating on her—or at least thinking about it—I don't think that boy has much of a leg to stand on."

"Interesting." And it actually *is* interesting. Because it almost seems like Bristol has bought into this whole thing, like she actually believes Brianna's twisted reality.

"What's even more interesting is that you were the slut who was emailing Asher all this time. I didn't really believe it at first. When Brianna said she thought it was you, I told her she was wrong. But it seems I was the one who was wrong. You've obviously been hitting on him online for weeks now, sending him photos and promising to do all kinds of slutty things if he'll just break up with Brianna. I don't even know why I'm talking to you about this when I honestly can't stand to look at you."

"I don't know why you're talking to me either. But if you want to find out the real truth, you should talk to Asher. Ask him about those emails and how he felt when he was writing them."

"Right." She looks like she's ready to really tear into me now. "I'll just run down to city hall and do that."

"City hall?"

"Oh, yeah, the innocent act again. I suppose you didn't know that Asher was just picked up by the police—right in front of the whole school. You didn't see that, did you? Not that it would bother you much, being a jailbird and all yourself. And I'm sure you didn't have anything to do with his arrest either."

Okay, this one catches me off guard. But I maintain my poker face and just study her. She seems genuinely upset by this latest development, which convinces me that she really doesn't know the truth. I mean, she's into drama and all that, but this seems very real. It's like she's worried about Asher and trying to protect Brianna. Sweet, but sad.

"You really make me sick, Elise. You're a disease—like swine flu. You come into our school and you contaminate everything you touch. We even tried to befriend you, which was total stupidity, and this is how you thank us. You stab Brianna in the back, you try to steal her boyfriend. And then when that doesn't work out, you turn him in to the police and accuse him of . . . what exactly? He gets arrested on the day of the homecoming dance, almost like you planned it from the start—like if you can't have him, no one can. You should see how devastated Brianna is right now. No, you shouldn't see . . . because you wouldn't care. You'd probably just laugh. Seriously, why don't you just go back to wherever it was you crawled out—"

"That's enough," Phillip says quietly.

"And you!" Bristol says to him as she gathers her things. "I don't know how you can stand to be around her, but I'm done. I refuse to be exposed to her disgusting filth anymore. She's worse than a disease—she's a monster." Bristol storms off to a solitary table in the back of the room.

"Good riddance," Katie says quietly.

I blink in surprise. "You don't like her?"

Katie shakes her head.

"But you sit with her?"

"She sits with me."

Phillip chuckles. "I think Bristol was hoping artistic talent might rub off, and since you're the best around, she chose to sit by you."

Katie gives him a half smile.

I settle back down to work, but my hands are too shaky for pen and ink today. Instead I go back to pencil sketching, trying to duplicate a photo of a lonely old shack in the middle of a scrubby field.

As I sketch, I try to remember that Bristol wasn't *really* talking about me when she said all those mean things. She doesn't even know who I am. Not really. She was talking about the person Brianna has tried to make me out to be—a fictional character who would be a monster if she really existed. I realize again that Bristol's venom was her way of showing loyalty to a friend she believes I've betrayed. I just hope it won't be long until the truth comes out. Otherwise, I might start to believe that I really am the one to blame for this big mess.

16

Phillip and I are out in the school parking lot, making last-minute plans for the dance tonight.

"I'll pick you up at 6:30," he tells me. "I actually got a reservation for us at L'astrance for 7:15."

I blink in astonishment. I've heard my mom mention this French restaurant before—as in it's fantastic but hard to get into. "No way! You got us in there? How is that even possible?"

He grins. "With God all things are possible."

"Wow, your connection to him must be stronger than mine."

"Actually, my mom's best friend is the owner." He smiles sheepishly.

"Hey, whatever, that's awesome. So see you at 6:30. I better get moving since I have a lot to do before then."

Phillip waits as I unlock my car. That's when I notice Brianna and her girlfriends watching me from where they're huddled next to a white convertible. I could be paranoid, but I'm sure they're talking about me. And if looks could kill, I would be toast.

As I reach to open my door, I notice the key gash through the paint again, which gives me an idea. I point to the scar on Bonnie Blue, peering at Brianna with a questioning expression. Brianna just laughs. I exchange glances with Phillip, and it's plain he gets it too.

"I'm surprised she could see the scratch from that distance," I say as I open my door and get inside. "But she seems to think it's funny."

"I'm surprised the poor girl is actually laughing," he adds sarcastically. "Considering how devastated she is over Asher's unfortunate incarceration."

"I'm glad you witnessed that," I say as I start the engine.

"Don't forget about how keys can retain paint fragments."

I nod. "See you later." As I drive away, I wish I had my cell phone to call Wally and give him my latest information. Not only about the car, but perhaps to help vindicate Asher, because I'm starting to believe he's actually been the victim of circumstances, or just the victim of bad taste in girlfriends. As it is, I am phone-less, so it will have to wait.

I meet Grandma as planned in the formal wear department of Macy's. "I picked out a few things that you might like," she tells me. "Although I suspect you'll have your own ideas."

"Actually, I have no ideas," I confess. "That I'm even going to this dance still feels unreal." We go back to the fitting rooms where a woman has been helping Grandma, and I'm pleasantly surprised to see that I actually like a couple of the dresses they've picked out. The ones that just aren't me, I hand back.

"You try them on," the saleswoman tells me, "and I'll do some more looking around for styles and colors that are similar to the ones you like. It appears you go more for classic styles . . . and not too fussy."

"Yes, I've never been too much into the princess thing," I admit.

Between trying on dresses in various styles, colors, and sizes, I manage to squeeze in a break to call Wally on Grandma's phone. "I don't know that there's much you can do about this," I tell him, "but I've learned some things today that strongly suggest Brianna Cole is at the bottom of most of this." I tell him what Bristol revealed about the email, and also about how Brianna laughed when I pointed to the scratch on my car, explaining how she was too far away to actually see it. "But Phillip told me there could be traces of my paint in her keys."

"Phillip is right."

"It's not like I'm trying to get her locked up, but the repair work on my car is probably going to be expensive and—"

"No kidding. And if that girl is behind all of these things, she deserves to be locked up for a while."

"Instead of Asher," I tell him. "I could tell he was clueless about most of this when we talked today."

Wally thanks me for the tips and promises to do what he can to investigate them. "Have fun at the dance."

"I'll do my best," I say, realizing that Phillip and I will probably be less than welcome by a number of people there. I wonder if this store carries dresses with bulletproof bodices.

Instead I decide on a silvery gray dress that Grandma says looks great with my eyes and skin tone. "You really do have a lovely tan," she tells me as I model the final selection for her and the saleslady.

"Hopefully you're using sunblock for those UV rays," the woman says.

I give a sheepish grin. "Sometimes."

She just shakes her head. "Young girls these days."

It's a little after five by the time I've picked out a dress and shoes and we're on our way to our cars. I hug Grandma in the parking lot, telling her that I better get home if I want to be ready for Phillip at 6:30. "I don't even know how to thank you for everything," I tell her. "I feel like I'm Cinderella and you're my fairy godmother."

She chuckles. "Fairy *grand*mother is more like it. Just make sure your mom gets some photos tonight. By the way, she said she'd be home in time to see you off." She waves goodbye.

I promise her the photos, but then as I'm driving home, I realize Mom and I are still camera-less. Perhaps Stacie will let me borrow hers . . . if she's talking to me, that is. Although, knowing Stacie, if she sees me dressed up for the dance, she will probably warm up out of pure curiosity. Plus, seeing me participating in a normal event might help convince her that I'm not exactly the pariah she imagines me to be. And maybe I can explain that this whole ugly mess might be coming to an end, and that we're narrowing in on the real guilty parties now. That should help to relieve her mind about me.

Just a little past six, I'm dressed and mostly ready, although I'm not sure what to do with my hair. First I try it up, then down, and finally up again. Mom's not home to give her opinion, but I decide to find out if I can borrow a camera and see what Stacie thinks in regard to my hair.

"Wow," she says when she opens the door. "What's up with you?"

"I'm going to the homecoming dance with Phillip," I tell her.

"Oh."

"And I promised my grandma that we'd get a picture, but our cameras are kind of confiscated, you know. Do you think I could borrow one?"

She frowns now.

"I'll bring it right back," I promise her.

"The problem is the battery's dead," she tells me.

"My mom might have a battery."

"And I think the memory card is full."

"Okay, fine," I tell her. "I get it. You're still freezing me out. Even though my attorney is getting ready to prove that these nasty allegations against me are totally false, you're still holding—"

"How's he going to prove that?"

"He's been collecting evidence."

"When will you know for sure . . . I mean that you're innocent?"

"I know I'm innocent right now!"

"I mean when will your name be cleared—like will it go to court?"

"It sounds like we can get my charges dismissed. Maybe by early next week if all goes well." I glance down to the parking lot, spotting Mom hurrying out of her car. "My attorney's got more evidence and stuff. It's looking pretty good for me."

"Oh." She nods. "That's great."

"Well, I better go finish getting ready."

"Sorry about the camera," she says as she closes the door.

"Elise!" Mom exclaims as I meet her at the top of the stairs. "You look absolutely gorgeous!"

"Thank you!" I do a little spin for her then open our front door.

"You'll be the belle of the ball."

I control the urge to roll my eyes. "Well, at least I'll be there." We go inside, and I quickly fill her in on the latest developments of the case.

"It sounds like Asher and Brianna might not make this dance together after all." She puts the last pin in my hair, which we decided looks best up. "Ironic, isn't it? Considering that seemed to be what all the fuss was about in the first place."

"I don't know. Brianna is a very driven person." I follow Mom to her room, where she pulls her jewelry box out of a drawer. "I'll bet that girl's not above breaking Asher out of jail just to have him take her to the dance."

Mom laughs as she lifts the lid, then she turns back to me with her beautiful diamond earrings in her hand—the ones Grandpa gave her when she turned thirty a few years ago. "I think that dress needs these, don't you, Elise?"

"Seriously?" I stare at the sparkling solitaires. "You're not worried I'll lose one?"

"They have screw-on backs." She shows me. "Almost impossible to lose."

She helps me put them on and then we check them out in the mirror. "This feels kind of surreal," I admit. "Like just a few nights ago I was sitting there in our bathroom thinking about knocking myself off and—"

"*What?*" Mom looks horrified.

"I'm sorry. I didn't mean to say that."

"Is it true?"

I explain about my dark night—the day of the arrest—and how I poured all her sleeping pills into my hand. "I'm sorry," I say again. "I wasted them."

"You wasted them?"

"By dumping them down the toilet."

She looks relieved.

"They'd gotten all clumped together in my sweaty hand and I don't think—"

"You didn't waste them, Elise. That was the right thing to do." She hugs me. "I'm so thankful you had good sense. And I'm so sorry I was being such a poor excuse of a mother then."

We hear knocking on the door, and I tell Mom about my promise to get pictures for Grandma. "But we don't have cameras and Stacie wouldn't—"

"Oh yes we do," she says as she grabs up her purse. "I picked up a disposable during lunch today."

I open the door to Phillip, and his eyes light up when he sees me. "Wow!" He nods with approval. "You look stunning!"

"Thanks. Same back at you. That tux is great."

He holds out a flat package wrapped in brown paper and tied with a piece of string. "It's not flowers," he says with a twinkle in his eye.

"No, I didn't think so."

"I just didn't know what kind of flowers to get," he admits. "And my sister told me that not everyone does flowers. Anyway, I'd been wanting to give you this since Monday."

"Should I open it?"

He nods.

It turns out to be the drawing of Jesus's hand, neatly matted and framed. "Wow," I say as I admire his work. "Do you really want me to have this?"

"Absolutely."

"Thank you! I love it!" I show it to Mom. "It's Jesus's hand," I explain. "Phillip drew it."

"You're quite an artist," Mom tells him. "And now, if you don't mind, I promised Elise's grandmother that we'd take some photos."

I strike some poses with Phillip, who looks dashing in his retro tux, and Mom takes about a dozen shots. "You kids have fun," she finally tells us as we're leaving.

"Did I tell you that you look stunning?" Phillip asks as he opens the car door for me.

"Yes, you mentioned that already. But thank you."

"Thank *you*!"

The parking lot nearest the restaurant looks packed, so Phillip decides to splurge for valet parking instead. "This is more elegant anyway," he tells me as he pulls right up to the front of the restaurant. "It goes with how you look."

As he's helping me out of his car, we notice a stretch Hummer pulling in behind us. A bunch of kids in formal wear start spilling out, kind of like the clown car in the circus, one after the next. Among them are Brianna and Asher and the rest of their friends. Suddenly my heart is pounding and it's like my silver sandals have been superglued to the pavement—because I'm actually afraid to move. I just stand and watch as the group pauses to glare at us and then backs away like we're contagious. Then, haughtily, they turn away, and the circus parade funnels into the restaurant.

"Come on," Phillip says quietly as he takes my elbow in his hand and escorts me toward the entrance. "Don't let them rattle you."

"I won't," I promise. "It just took me by surprise."

Now their noisy, colorful group is glommed around the reservation desk and filling up the small foyer. But Phillip eases past them and gives his name to the hostess, and just like that we're being led into the restaurant. I control myself from letting out a cheer. I so didn't want to stand out there and wait among them. We're quickly led to a delightful corner table near the fountain area, where we're seated and given menus.

"Do you think they'll be eating in a banquet room?" I say quietly after the hostess leaves.

He chuckles. "L'astrance doesn't have a banquet room."

Somehow the restaurant accommodates the group at several tables in the center of the room. Although I try not to watch, it doesn't appear that they're getting the level of service we are. I overhear Brianna complaining about the location of the table as well as the wait.

Just as we're finishing up our entrées, which are amazing, a beautiful older woman in a sleek black dress comes out, and Phillip introduces her to me as Yvonne, the owner of the restaurant.

"A pleasure to meet you, Elise," Yvonne tells me. "Phillip's mother is my dearest friend in the whole wide world. As well as the person who encouraged me to start my own restaurant." She smiles down at Phillip. "Naturally, we like to accommodate our dear friends when we can."

"Everything was absolutely delicious," I tell her. I can hear how quiet the other tables have gotten—as if everyone in the restaurant is watching us.

"And if you don't mind"—Yvonne winks at Phillip—"I've arranged for a complimentary dessert for you."

"That sounds great." He nods and she waves back to the kitchen area, where a chef emerges with a silver cart and parks it by our table. He proceeds to put together a concoction of berries and brandy, which he lights on fire—and everyone exclaims over—then he ladles this over a delicate piece of cake and tops it with some kind of cream.

"C'est le bon," Yvonne says to Phillip. "Enjoy!"

"Thank you," he tells her. "Everything was spectacular tonight."

She nods toward me with a smile. "Including your date."

I thank her for everything, then she tells us to have fun at the dance. "And remember, you're only young once!"

I feel like royalty as Phillip and I are served this amazing dessert with a French name I can't begin to pronounce. We finish it off with tiny cups of espresso. I think that even if we didn't go to the dance afterward, it would still be a perfect evening.

"This feels like a fairy tale," I tell Phillip as we're finishing up. "I mean compared to how my week started out . . . well, it's just unbelievable. Thank you so much for asking me out tonight."

"Thank you for coming. I'm enjoying it too."

"And Yvonne was so sweet."

"I think we were the envy of the restaurant."

I try not to feel too smug . . . but it is a nice little turn-about.

"I don't want to make you uncomfortable," he says quietly, "but we've been watched tonight."

"I tried not to notice."

He chuckles. "Brianna looked seriously ticked when she saw Yvonne come to our table."

"I can't believe they're here tonight," I admit. "I mean Asher and Brianna *together*. Especially after what I heard today—and then Asher's arrest—and with him knowing what she did. Well, it's a little surprising, don't you think?"

He nods. "Yes, the plot just keeps thickening."

Finally our coffees and dessert are done. Phillip takes care of the bill and we are on our way to the dance. When we get there, I'm feeling pretty nervous. I'm not even sure why. I mean, really, what could possibly happen—well, besides anything?

None of Asher and Brianna's crowd has arrived yet. Phillip and I actually enjoy several dances, and I begin to relax and think maybe the others decided not to come. In that case, this could be a very fun evening. I decide, hands down, that

Phillip is the perfect date. Honestly, I wonder what I ever saw in Asher in the first place—besides an illusion.

I'm just thinking this is going to be the best night of my life when the snob squad arrives.

I can feel a shift of mood in the entire ballroom as their "elite" group makes their noisy entrance—like they think they're royalty or entitled or just spoiled brats. Everyone else gets slightly uneasy and uncomfortable . . . or maybe it's just my imagination. But the atmosphere feels different. And when these kids start dancing, it's like the rest of us automatically move back a few feet, making room for them, like we all know this crowd will settle for nothing less than center stage.

Phillip and I dance a few more songs, but the fun factor seems to have totally evaporated for me, plus I need to use the restroom—and not to powder my nose either. So while everyone is dancing to a popular song, I slip out, and thankfully there is no one in the restroom.

I go clear down to the end stall but soon realize it's a challenge to maneuver a long dress with slippery layers in order to use the toilet. I really don't want any part of this pretty dress taking a dip. After several attempts, I finally figure out that if I slide the dress up around my torso and then pull the skirt higher, hoisting it over my shoulder and anchoring it with one arm, I can actually use the toilet without endangering my gown.

I've just sat down when I hear voices—familiar ones—entering the restroom. And for some reason—maybe even fear—I decide to lift my feet up so it looks like no one's in this stall. Sitting there with my dress hiked over my shoulder and both feet planted solidly on the door, I just wait, hoping they won't be in here too long.

"I can't believe that slut would show her face tonight," Brianna says. I can see through the crack in the door that they're clustered in front of the large mirror touching up their makeup. "I wish someone would lock her up and throw away the key."

Lindsey chuckles. "They probably will before long."

"I noticed Asher looking at her in the restaurant," Bristol says. "Are you sure he's over her?"

Brianna cusses. "Of course he's over her. He thinks she's certifiable."

"Chance told me that Asher and the slut had a nice little talk today," Lindsey says in a slightly catty tone.

"*What?*" Brianna sounds furious. "When did this happen? Why didn't you tell me?"

"I'm not supposed to." Lindsey giggles, and something about her makes me think she's been drinking.

"Lindsey." Brianna's voice softens now. "You're my friend. Why wouldn't you tell me about this?"

"I don't really see why it matters," Lindsey says. "Everyone's going to know sooner or later anyway."

"Going to know *what* sooner or later?" Brianna persists.

"You know, Brianna, *about the emails.*" Lindsey's voice is definitely slushy. "That's all they were talking about."

"You mean Asher and Elise were talking about the emails?" Brianna asks.

"Yesh."

Brianna lets out another foul word. For some reason it seems such a contrast to her appearance—sweet face, wide eyes, petite figure dressed in a delicate blue dress . . . almost angelic looking. Go figure.

"*What* about the emails?" Bristol asks.

"You know," Lindsey tells her. "Everyone knows."

"Knows what?" Bristol presses her.

"That they were faked by—"

"*Lindsey.*" Brianna's voice is still soft, but there's a sharp edge to it. "Hey, Bristol, can I borrow your lip gloss? It's such a great color and mine is all—"

"What do you mean they were faked?" Bristol asks Lindsey. "Who faked them anyway?"

Lindsey laughs. "Serioushly, Bristol, you dunno who faked 'em?"

"Lindsey, I think you're confused," Brianna says quickly. "Not to mention sloshed. Just how many Cosmos did you put away at Bristol's house anyway?"

"I want to know what's going on," Bristol says in a firm voice. "You two are keeping something from me—now give."

"It's nothing," Brianna says. "Let's get back out there before that slut puts the move on one of our boyfriends. Better watch out, Bristol, I'm pretty sure I saw her looking at Hayward. She's probably going after—"

"No," Bristol interrupts. "I want the truth first."

I'm about ready to bust out of there and tell her the truth—or what I suspect is the truth—but somehow I think it will be better coming from the source. Better for everyone. I actually bow my head and silently pray now, begging God to bring the truth to light.

"Jus' tell her," Lindsey urges. "No big deal."

"I want to go dance," Brianna says in an irritated voice.

"Not yet." Through the crack in the door, I can see Bristol moving, and I'm guessing she's blocking Brianna's exit. "Tell me who faked the email first."

"I'll tell you," Lindsey announces. "Brianna faked it. And she did a good job of it too. She pretended to be Asher and strung loser girl along, acting like she, I mean *he*, was in love with Elise. Brianna even got the slut to send photos, and she had this plan—" Lindsey laughs hard, like this is hilarious. I'm guessing Brianna is right—Lindsey probably did drink too much. "And all the time Brianna was going to blackmail her, and the slut's such a dope, she fell for it."

"Shut up, Lindsey," Brianna snaps.

"Is that true, Brianna?" Bristol's voice is icy. "Did you set Elise up like that? Pretending to be Asher?"

"What if I did?"

"And all the while you were telling me about how Elise was chasing after him?" Bristol continues. I'm thinking this girl is so smart she could probably be a great attorney. "But you were really after Elise right from the start, weren't you?"

Brianna chuckles. "Pretty brilliant, don't you think?"

"Pretty low-down mean, I'd say."

"Hey, who died and made you Mother Teresa?"

"I told you about what happened to my friend in middle school." Bristol sounds tightly wound now. "I told you that whole horrible story. About what those girls did to Rachel Snyder. I told you about how she killed herself because she couldn't take it anymore. I told you how much I hate that kind of thing, Brianna. And then you lied to me about the emails— you lied to me about Elise! What is wrong with you?"

The room is quiet, and I think everyone has heard enough. Including me. I stand up, flush the toilet, rearrange my dress, open the door, and step out. All three of them stare at me like I'm an apparition. Pretending to ignore them, I simply wash my hands, dry them, and wad and toss the towel. Then I look directly at Bristol.

"I'm really sorry about your friend Rachel," I tell her in a sincere tone. "My friend Hilary told me about what happened in middle school. And I can personally relate to how Rachel must've felt. As sad as it is, I understand why she couldn't take it anymore. Without God's help, I would've given up too."

Then I just walk out.

17

"Wait," Bristol calls out as Phillip and I are getting ready to leave the dance. It seems to me that the fun is over. But we both turn and wait as Bristol rushes toward us. "What you said in the restroom about Rachel," she says breathlessly. "That was true, wasn't it?"

"I never actually knew Rachel, but Hilary told me about her. And what I said about relating to her was totally true."

She puts her hand on my arm and looks directly at me. "Elise, I'm so sorry."

I actually feel tears coming to my eyes now.

"I'm sorry on so many accounts," she continues. "I'm sorry I thought the worst about you. I'm sorry I tore into you today. I'm sorry I believed Brianna's lies about you." She shakes her head. "Really, I am just so sorry."

"Thanks." I nod. "I believe you. And if it makes you feel any better, I had a feeling you were just fighting Brianna's battle for her—I mean her make-believe battle."

"But that nude photo?" Bristol frowns. "Brianna swears she did not send it. And for some reason I think she's telling the truth about this. I mean, yes, she obviously did everything else, which is so disgusting I don't even want to go there. But she swears she didn't send the photo, although she did confess to forwarding it from Asher's phone—"

"She admitted to forwarding it?"

Bristol nods. "Only after I interrogated her about everything. We were in there for a while after you left. But Brianna totally denies having anything to do with the nude photo. She even said she was surprised when you sent it from your phone, but she was happy that you caved."

"I didn't cave!"

"That photo isn't Elise," Phillip says. "And that's going to be proven by experts next week."

Bristol nods. "Okay, I can accept that. But *who* sent that photo?"

I am totally mystified. "I was convinced that Brianna did. I even thought that maybe you and Lindsey helped her to pull it off."

"I didn't. And I honestly don't think Lindsey did either."

"Oh . . ."

"Anyway, I told Brianna that either she confesses the truth to Asher or I do. She said she's going to tell him everything tonight. But I plan to follow it up, just in case."

"I appreciate that."

"Are you guys leaving?"

I glance at Phillip then shrug. "I thought it might be best."

"Don't go," she urges us. "That makes it look like Brianna won."

Phillip nods. "Good point."

"You guys look so great tonight. And it seemed like you were having a good time. Please, don't go because of Brianna."

A part of me feels like this could be a trick. Seriously, what a switch from Art class today. But then I remember the conversation in the restroom . . . and I feel certain I can trust Bristol now.

"Come on," Bristol urges me. "Stay and have fun. And I promise I'll follow up Brianna's confession with Asher."

Phillip looks at me. "You want to stay?"

I nod, so we stay. As we're dancing, I see Asher and Brianna hashing it out over in a corner. Asher looks seriously angry, so I suspect Brianna really is confessing. But it is reassuring when Bristol and her boyfriend Hayward go over and join them. It's like having *The People's Court* at the homecoming dance. I'm just glad I don't have to go over there and testify myself.

Before the dance is over, Asher brings Brianna over to where Phillip and I are taking a break. "Brianna has something to say to you, Elise," he tells me in a serious tone.

Brianna won't even look at me. I can tell this is going to be a forced apology, which seems pretty juvenile and ridiculous.

"Come on," he tells her, "you promised."

"Fine." She looks up. "I'm sorry."

"That was real heartfelt," he says.

"It's the best I can do at the moment."

Asher shrugs. "And I'm sorry too, Elise. Sorry that I fell for Brianna's lies about you. You didn't deserve any of this."

"So what happens next?" Phillip asks him. "It's cool that you guys—well, at least you—apologized. But what about the criminal charges against Elise?"

"I plan to tell the police the truth," Asher says.

"But we're not taking the blame for that nasty photo," Brianna says quickly. "I didn't do that, and I'm willing to take a lie detector test if necessary to prove it." She glares at me now. "You might've convinced Bristol and Asher that photo wasn't of you and that you didn't send it, but I don't believe you."

"Believe what you want," I say. "The truth will come out."

"And you did *forward* the photo," Phillip reminds her. "We know that for sure."

She frowns.

"And you sent those fake emails," I add. "Some of those will be pretty incriminating." I stare at her, still in partial disbelief that someone with such an innocent face could be so mean-spirited. "And you did all that just to hold on to Asher?"

"Not that it's working," Asher says in a tired voice. "Now, I'm going home, Brianna. You can ride with me or stay here. I don't really care."

Looking slightly whipped, she goes with him. I can only

imagine the conversation they'll have on the way home. I'm pretty sure she'll try to convince him that she only did all this because she loves him, because she was looking out for his best interests, trying to protect him from me . . . whatever. But I'm sure she'll try to spin it toward her own best interests.

Phillip and I stay for the duration of the dance. We even sit and visit with Bristol and Hayward for a while. I think both of them are really quite nice. And Bristol is actually the kind of girl I'd love to have for a good friend.

I think everyone is learning (or starting to learn) a lesson from all this. I hope so anyway. But as Phillip drives me home, I am plagued with one nagging question—if Brianna really didn't do it, then who is responsible for that photo?

18

I sleep in on Saturday, but when I wake up it's such a gorgeous, sunny day—just like summer—I decide to go down by the tiny apartment pool and just relax while I read a paperback. I have to admit it feels a bit lonely down there—and I really do miss having Stacie around to joke with—but I decide not to obsess over it.

Instead, I'm obsessing over the photo question—asking myself over and over what other enemies I can possibly have. Who could hate me that much? Who would stoop to such nastiness? Besides the whole Brianna crowd, which seems fairly cleared, I honestly can't think of anyone. It's just too weird. But if I can just prove I'm not the girl in the photo, at least I can put this thing to rest. Or so I hope.

I hear footsteps and notice Stacie's sister walking through the courtyard around the pool, probably coming to beg money from her poor mom again. According to Stacie, this is the usual reason for Leslie's sporadic and brief visits.

Then suddenly it hits me.

Leslie looks a lot like me. Both Stacie and her mom have pointed this out more than once. As I watch Leslie going up the stairs, I realize that they're right. We're about the same height, same build, same hair length and color—seriously, one of us could be a stand-in if the other one was starring in a film. Except for one thing.

I stand up and follow Leslie, calling out to her, "Hey, wait a minute."

She turns and looks at me. "Oh, Elise, I didn't see you there. What's up?"

"Just catching some sun." I lift my sunglasses and squint at her.

"Using your sunscreen, I hope."

I force a laugh. "Oh, you know me, I go for the low SPF numbers."

"Then you'll probably look like dried-up beef jerky by the time you're my age," she says.

I nod. "Maybe so. I'll bet you never go out in the sun without sunscreen."

"I never go out in the sun—period."

"Right . . ." The skanky image of the nude, pale-skinned girl feels like it's been indelibly imprinted into my brain so that, even as I'm talking to her, I can see it. "I want to talk to Stacie. Mind if I follow you in?" I ask as she opens their door.

Now she gives me a slightly suspicious look. Ignoring her, I push right past, nodding at their mom, who is in her usual position on the couch with the TV blaring. "Stacie," I call out, "where are you?"

Stacie emerges from her bedroom with a curious expression. "What's going—"

"We need to talk," I tell her. I pick up the remote from the coffee table and turn off the TV.

Their mom stares at me. "What are you do—"

"You need to hear this," I tell her. I point to Stacie and Leslie. "You both sit down."

As they do, I proceed to tell their mother about what happened to me, how someone sent a photo and said it was me, but she interrupts. "I know all about that nasty little incident," she says with a wave of her hand.

"You know *all* about it?" I demand.

"Oh, sure, Stacie told me the whole thing."

"The whole thing?" I glance at Stacie and can tell by her expression that she didn't tell her mother *every*thing. "That photo of the nude girl," I say, "was a photo of Leslie, and—"

"What?" Their mother's eyes grow wide. "Are you crazy?"

"No, but apparently your daughters might be."

"What are you saying?" She narrows her eyes at me.

"I'm saying that your daughters are not who you think they are." I pause to look at both Stacie and Leslie now. Their faces pretty much proclaim their guilt. Not that Leslie seems overly concerned. If anything, she's amused. But I use this dramatic break to reconstruct what happened—how it went down, the order of events. Not that it takes a genius to figure it out. "And I'm saying that Stacie," I continue slowly, "who is always getting into my purse and going through my things like she thinks she's my little sister . . . I'm suggesting that Stacie snatched my phone. And she somehow talked Leslie into—"

"Try *bribed*," Leslie offers with a sly smile. "Money talks, you know."

"Fine, Stacie *bribed* Leslie to pose nude, and Stacie snapped a photo on my phone and then sent it to Asher's phone. Thanks to Asher's jealous girlfriend, that photo got forwarded to the whole school, and I got arrested on child porn charges. And that's why Stacie has been avoiding me like the plague for the past week. Right?" I ask Stacie.

Now she's crying. She buries her head in her hands and just starts sobbing. She shakes her head and mutters, "I'm sorry, I'm sorry," over and over again.

"Is that true?" their mom demands of Leslie.

"Hey, I didn't know what was going on," Leslie tells her. "Stacie told me she was going to do a favor for someone, and she offered me ten bucks to—"

"Get out of here," her mom yells at Leslie.

"Hey, don't blame me, I was just—"

"Get out!" Her mom points to the door. "Stacie is *fourteen* years old. What on earth do you think you're doing posing in the nude for a fourteen-year-old to photograph? Don't come back here until you can grow up."

"Fine!" Leslie yells as she grabs her purse. She pauses to glare at me like I'm the spoiler in her little game. "I won't come back—ever!"

"I'm sorry," I say to Stacie's mom. "But I had to get to the bottom of this. I was arrested and I need to clear my—"

"You're not the one who should be sorry," her mom says.

"I said I'm sorry," Stacie tells us both with red-rimmed eyes. "I'm really sorry. I wanted to tell you the truth, Elise, but I didn't know how. I never knew it would turn out like it did. And then it just got worse and worse."

"All I want to know is *why*." I watch her face. "What made you do it?"

"Because I saw how much you loved Asher—"

"But that's no reason to—"

"I could tell how much he liked you. And I thought you'd get him if you just sent him one photo. I thought for sure he'd dump Brianna if he could see how hot you are."

"You mean how hot Leslie is," I correct her.

"You know what I mean." She takes in a shaky breath. "I thought I was helping you. You were so worried that it was over—that he wasn't going to email you anymore and—"

"But what you didn't know—or me either at the time—was that Brianna was the one writing those emails."

"No way!"

"It was Brianna the whole time. She pretended to be Asher to keep me away from him. It was her way of keeping us apart. And you sending that photo played right into her hands."

"I'm sorry, Elise!"

Her mom is shaking her head hopelessly. "How did I manage to raise two total idiots for daughters?"

"She's not an idiot," I say in defense of Stacie. "But she was foolish and immature, and she fell into a trap and dragged me along with her."

"I'm so, so sorry," she mutters again.

"I know you are," I tell her. "But I blame Leslie even more than you. She's older, she should've known better."

Her mom just laughs, but it's not a happy laugh.

I ignore her. "I understand that you thought you were helping me, Stacie, but you have to see how stupid that was—"

"I do see. And I'll never do anything like that again." She wipes her wet cheeks with the sleeve of her shirt. "Do you think I'll be arrested now?"

I consider this. "Well, I'm not sure how they define child porn exactly. I mean Leslie's not a child . . . but you are."

She just nods.

"If I were you, I'd go turn myself in to the police. Just confess what you did and get it over with. I have a feeling given your age and your sister's age . . . well, they'll probably go lightly on you. They told me if I'd confess—even though I didn't do it—that I'd probably just have to do community service and take a class or something."

She nods and her mom groans.

"You better take her in," I warn Stacie's mom. "The sooner the better." I turn to leave.

"Elise?" Stacie calls out in a meek voice.

"Yeah?"

"Will you ever forgive me?"

I turn and give her a long look. "Yeah. I have to forgive you because that's what God did for me." A jolt of reality hits me, and I know Stacie isn't the only one at fault here. "And you'll have to forgive me too," I tell her.

"Forgive *you*?" Her eyes grow wide. "What for?"

"I wasn't honest with you this summer. I made it sound like I'd had a lot of boyfriends and stuff. The truth is I've never had a real boyfriend . . . and I've never been kissed."

"No way!" She looks stunned.

"It's true." I nod. "Sorry I lied to you. It seemed like no big deal back then. But I realize now that I could've set you up to think I was someone I'm not. Maybe that's why you thought it was okay to send that photo."

"That still doesn't make sending that photo okay," her mom points out angrily.

"I know, Mom." Stacie presses her lips together then looks back at me. "So do you mean it, can you really forgive me for that?"

"Yeah. But how about if I make a deal with you? Kind of like a form of penance, okay?"

"Sure, whatever. Want me to clean your room? Do your chores? You name it—as long as it doesn't involve photography."

I laugh. "Trust me, it has nothing to do with photographs. Here's the deal, Stacie. I'll forgive you, and in return, you have to come to church with me for . . . let's see, how about one day for one day."

"Huh?"

"Well, I've been through six days—some of them were pretty rough days too. Six long days of being considered guilty of something I didn't do. You go to church with me for six Sundays and I think we'll be okay."

She brightens. "Okay."

"Now," her mom says, "get your shoes on, Stacie. I think Elise is right. The sooner we take care of this, the better."

Life settles down the following week. At least for me. Thanks to Stacie and Bristol, all charges against me are dropped. But Stacie, as predicted, is sentenced to community service, which includes removing graffiti from public restrooms and speaking to middle school students about why sexting is really, really stupid, not to mention illegal. She's also sentenced to going to church with me, which she admits after the first time isn't so bad.

Brianna, I learn from Bristol, could've had a similar light sentence if she'd simply agreed to it. Of course, Brianna decided not to own up to everything she'd already confessed to her friends and Asher. Now she's hired an attorney and plans to appeal. Wally is trying to get an out-of-court settlement from Brianna's parents for the damage to my car, which Lindsey (thanks to Bristol) told me she witnessed.

Asher's name is cleared as well, but he and Brianna are history. And even though he's been unusually friendly to me, I am keeping him at a cool distance. It's not that I question his sincerity—I simply question his judgment. I mean what kind of a boy goes with a girl like Brianna for that long without figuring out what she's really like?

Anyway, Phillip isn't like that. From what I can see, Phillip has good judgment and he genuinely cares about me. And those might be rare qualities in seventeen-year-old boys these days. Not that I'm an expert. Although I am getting smarter.

Among the many things that I learned through all this mess is that crushes are usually misleading. It's like I'd set myself up to believe whatever it was I wanted to believe about Asher because I'd convinced myself I was madly in love with him—and trust me, that's asking for trouble. Because, think about it, when I thought I was falling for Asher, I was actually corresponding with Brianna. Ugh, how sick is that?

That's what the internet is like sometimes—you think you know who you're talking to, but sometimes you don't. For one thing, you can't hear the tone of the person's voice to know whether it's sincere or not, and you can't see into a person's eyes to know if they're stringing you along. Even if a guy sends a cool photo, you can't be sure it's really him. You could actually be a scam victim like me . . . or worse.

But I've decided that even being scammed was partially my fault for playing along—and for being dishonest with Stacie.

I have to admit that I made myself a willing participant when I went for the bait—hook, line, and sinker, as they say. I set myself up for a great big fall. Really, I can't blame everyone else without blaming myself as well. No one forced me to play along.

So I may be only sixteen now, but already I'm a whole lot smarter than I was at fifteen. And even though I still haven't been officially kissed, I'm thinking that maybe I need to just wait.

Now, you probably think I mean I'll be waiting for Phillip . . . and who knows, that might be how it goes someday. The truth is I don't really know that part for sure.

What I'm actually saying is that I need to just wait *on God*. Because I know now that his timing and his ways are a whole lot better than mine!

Melody Carlson is the award-winning author of around two hundred books, many of them for teens, including the Diary of a Teenage Girl series, the TrueColors series, and the Carter House Girls series. She and her husband met years ago while volunteering as Young Life counselors. Visit Melody's website at www.melodycarlson.com.

Aster Flynn Wants a Life of Her Own . . .

But will her family get in her way?

Revell
a division of Baker Publishing Group
www.RevellBooks.com

Available wherever books are sold.

Girls know all about keeping secrets,
but Sophie's is a really big one.

Visit Melody Carlson at www.melodycarlson.com.

Come Meet Melody at
www.MelodyCarlson.com

- Enter a contest for a signed book
- Read her monthly newsletter
- Find a special page for book clubs
- And much more

Become a fan on Facebook
f Melody Carlson Books